Love's Stinging Bite

A. Kelly

PublishAmerica
Baltimore

Hardcover 978-1-4512-9367-8
Softcover 978-1-4512-9368-5
PUBLISHED BY PUBLISHAMERICA, LLLP
www.publishamerica.com
Baltimore

Printed in the United States of America

Prologue

It had seemed like an eternity had gone on, waging the underground war between vampires and lycans. No one knew when the next attack would happen. Only, when it did, the victim would remember no more. Only a sharp pain, then a howl of victory. All mortals were told to stay inside after hours, in order to keep them safe.

Thus, a rebellion was started. The time was modern day. Mortals worked alongside the vampires and lycans, struggling to try and maintain peace in the city, trying to keep all mortals safe. For if evil was to be let through, all mortals would fall, with nowhere to turn but to the shadows, where darkness would cover their hearts. Yes, mortals did know about the creatures, for it was the creatures that showed themselves to the mortals.

Yet, once again, night had fallen, with the full moon trying to pierce through the clouds. All mortals were being led back to their homes by soldiers, hoping to keep them safe, in case any enemy attacked, wishing to add more to their ranks. How long this has been going on, no one knows. But the knowledge of vampires and lycans had spread, making it easier for the darkness to find their prey.

One soldier waved to a pale woman, dressed in black garb, motioning the all clear sign over to her. She waved back, blue eyes narrowed, listening for sounds of the enemy. One twig snap or heavy footstep would alert them, and then the whole thing would come apart. A slithering sound next to her made her turn, eyes wide, breathing even. Nothing. A hand, claws unsheathed, started to swing down toward her.

The woman growled, eyes glowing yellow. She raised her right foot up, and kicked, knocking the creature back a few centimeters. It hit the ground hard, eyes seeing stars. The woman ran toward the soldier, hoping to get to him in time. A dark shadow rose up, racing after her. The soldier turned around, eyes wide.

The creature grabbed her shoulders and threw her down, making her land hard, breathless, on her back. It roared, aiming for the kill. The woman growled, kicking it in the jaw twice, making it stumble and growl. "Cursed lycans," She growled, "You've messed with the wrong hybrid!" She jumped up, pushing it back with the force of her palms. It let out a howl of surprise, landing hard against a building.

The lycan quickly bounced back, launching itself at the woman. Swiftly, it sank its teeth deep into her shoulder, tasting blood. The woman grabbed a hold of it, and tossed it aside.

The woman pulled her clawed hand back, about to kill the lycan, when the soldier grabbed her wrist, shaking his head, "Maybe we can help him. Get him on our side."

She looked up at him, swallowing a growl, then back to the lycan, too dazed to move. She sighed, "You're right." She got up off the lycan, brushing her hands off. She looked up at the soldier, "Call in a unit. Let's get this one back to base. Then call it a night. Seems like the enemy only wanted to test us."

He nodded, "Let's hope it was only that test. I shudder to think if there was more."

She smiled, "We'll see."

Not only were both sides trying to outdo the other. They were also coming up with ways to ensure the enemy's death. The rebels had it made, for they had created....a hybrid. A creature half vampire, and half lycan. Now, to make the rest of the rebel vampires and lycans to take this next step, and become something more.

The woman sighed, "Is this any way to get work done?"

Her partner looked at her, eyes narrowed, "Huh?"

She gave him a look, "Taking back wounded enemies, and trying to *change* them?" She shook her head, "It's just not right."

Her partner looked up at her, smiling, "It may not be right, but it's something we promised Lilth we would do." He grunted, finishing tying up the stilled beast, "Now, let's call that unit."

Chapter 1

Two girls ran through the darkened hallway, footsteps silent. Both were dressed in similar black garb. One had long, straight blonde hair pulled into a high ponytail. The other had long, flowing red hair, acting like a curtain flowing in the breeze. The blonde leapt up, hiding in the shadows above the door. She looked at the redhead, nodding. She nodded back, quickly opening the door, then hiding in the shadows, waiting for her partners' signal. The blonde jumped down, brushing the dust off of herself. She looked at the redhead, "You remember the mission, right?"

The redhead nodded, "Go in, snap some pics, and get out. Question is; do you remember the mission, Elora?"

Elora sighed, "C'mon, let's just get this over with." They slipped inside the room, keeping their eyes on the shadows for any movement. Elora smiled, "This seems to be the room. Got the camera ready?"

Asuka pulled out the camera, giving Elora a skeptical look, "And…what makes you think that this is the room?"

Elora shrugged, letting her eyes wander, "Gee, I don't know. It could be the fact that there are torches all around us, or the fact that there's an altar next to us. But those could be guesses, right? Just start snapping the pics so we could go!"

"Alright, alright," Asuka said, flicking on the switch, "I swear, you're so pushy." She looked over at her, "What does our boss want again?"

Elora sighed, "Just a few shots of the room. Nothing much."

"Can do," Asuka said, "Smile and say cheese!" She held up the camera, snapping away. She smiled, "Hey, Elora. I bet we'll get on the boss' good side after this."

"Yeah," Elora scoffed, "That is, if we even get to see the boss."

"Why don't we get to see him?" Asuka said, "Does he have something to hide?"

"Ugh, I don't know," Elora said. A noise made them both jump, "Um, Asuka? Can we hurry? I think the locals are onto us."

"Just one more....little snap," Asuka said, snapping the photo, "Yes! Let's go!" They took off out the door, running quickly. "Hurry!" Asuka exclaimed, "I think they're behind us!"

"No duh!" Elora exclaimed, breathless, "I think I see....a window up ahead. May....be....we can....jump outta it!" Elora sprinted forward, reaching for the sill. Asuka followed, close behind. Elora turned around, eyes wide, reaching out to her. Asuka reached out, fingers barely touching hers. "C'mon!" Elora exclaimed, "Reach!" Asuka tried, almost grasping her hand.

Something clawed and furry grasped her ankle, pulling her roughly back. Asuka cried out, fear immobilizing her body. She was flipped around, staring right into the face of a large, shaggy black wolf. It snarled, revealing rows and rows of sharp, glistening teeth.

"Thanner," A sharp voice called out, "Let her go." The black wolf sent the newcomer a look, before whimpering, letting go of Asuka. She sent the wolf a last panicked look, before scrambling away. She looked behind her, hoping Elora wasn't captured, but yet, hoping Elora would help her escape. Her jaw dropped. Someone was helping her back inside, a wide smile on his face. "Well," The voice said, "Hello, my dear. Welcome." Asuka turned around, eyes wide.

She took a few steps back, bumping into several people. She let out a small cry as they gripped her tightly, claws cutting sharply into her skin. She looked forward, squinting into the dark, "Show yourself!"

The figure laughed, stepping forward to the light, smiling wide. She moved a few strands of black hair out of her ivory white face, "Well now, you're a feisty one, aren't you?" She giggled, "I'm sure Xanatos will love you." She looked toward Elora, "It was a little soon to bring her here, but she'll do."

Asuka growled, looking over to Elora, "You set me up!"

Elora laughed, "Sorry, Asusu, but I was given a good offer that I simply couldn't refuse." She looked to the woman, "I knew Xanatos would love her, right, Star?"

Asuka felt her heart drop into her stomach, "Elora? Is this true? I'm…I'm…?"

Elora placed a finger on her lips, shushing her, "Now, child. Nothing personal, but it does get me in the boss's good graces."

Asuka growled, "You can't hold me here! I could fight all of you at once!"

Star bent down, looking into her face, "Dear, what kind of idiots do you take us for? What are we?" She bared her fangs, chuckling softly.

Asuka shied away, eyes wide, "V-Vampires."

Star smiled, "And we could kill you right now, if that is what you wish." Asuka shook her head, trying to keep the tears away.

Elora winked, "I'll let Xanatos know we have her."

Star nodded, "Right." She looked back at Asuka, her crimson eyes shining with triumph, "Let's get this one ready." She laughed, "Welcome to your new home, little one." Her laughter echoed in her ears, making her shake with fear. A cloth came over her nose, cutting off her breathing. She cried out, struggling, before finally falling to the ground, blacking out, and remembering no more.

**

It was late. Two figures stepped out of the shadows, eyes narrowed. One with silver hair stepped forward, a lazy smirk gracing his lips. "Well, Thane," He said, "Is the raid team assembled?"

"As they'll ever be," A figure with blonde hair said. He smirked, "This is gonna be some raid, Kursed."

Kursed smirked, mismatched eyes twinkling, "Of course. Tell the team to head in. We strike now."

"Right," Thane gestured to the shadows behind him, nodding. Yellow eyes glowed, acknowledging. The time was now.

***

Asuka awoke with a start, eyes wide. Slowly, she sat up, hearing a gong repeatedly going off inside her head. She groaned, holding her head. *'Ugh, what happened?'* She thought to herself, *'Oh yeah, I got kidnapped. Lovely. And did they really have to knock me out?'* She paused, trying to think of the right answer. She giggled to herself, *'Probably.'* She looked at herself, trying to see if anything was moved. Someone must have left her alone, for she was still wearing her black clothes. She sighed, *'Now, what to do?'* The doorknob turned, opening. She shied back, "Who's there? Show yourself!"

The figure laughed, "Elora and Star were both right. You are a feisty one." He stepped into the light. He was tall, very lean and muscular. Shaggy, jet black hair hung a little in his face, just barely over his eyes, which were silver. He looked her up and down. "Wow," He whispered, "You really are beautiful."

Asuka couldn't move, fear holding her down, "W-who are you?"

He laughed, "Forgive me, dear one. My name is Xanatos. And you," He took her hand gently in his and pulled her lightly off of the bed, kissing her hand gently, making her shake in fear, "Are now mine."

Asuka gave a nervous laugh, "Yeah, I think I'll be going now." She slipped around him, inching toward the door.

"You will not!" He hissed blocking her path and pinning her against the wall, "I've already chosen you." He smiled, fangs glinting in the light, "And now, you're mine." He bent down, stealing a kiss from her lips. Slowly, stealthily, he removed several hairs from her throat, clearing a space. She closed her eyes, feeling him move closer and closer, waiting for the pain.

A loud banging noise made Xanatos jerk up, growling in anger. He looked toward the door, eyes narrowed. "Stay here!" He barked, "We're not finished yet." She smiled. "And to make sure you stay…." He trailed of, holding his hand out, "Sleep." The word sounded like a hiss of a whisper, echoing in her mind. Asuka tried to keep her head up, eyes wide. She swayed slightly, before feeling her body fall, hitting the carpeted floor with a soft thumping sound. Xanatos growled, picking up Asuka and laying her on the bed, moving all hair from her face.

He lunged out the door, hearing the sounds of heavy footfalls racing past him. He reached out, grabbing one, "What's going on?"

"A raid sir!" The vampire said, "We're being attacked!"

Xanatos growled, "Get everyone in on it! Show those rebels no mercy!"

"Right!" The vampire saluted, "On it, sir!" Xanatos let go of him, watching him leave. He growled, hesitating, *Better go after him.* He took off, the hunt singing in his veins.

After some time, two figures stepped out of the shadows, Silver-hair running forward, right into the room, searching. The blonde one came up behind him, "Kursed?! What are you doing?!"

Kursed smirked, "Relax, Thane. You worry too much." He smirked, "I wanna see what Xanatos has in here that made him hesitate to leave this room." His eyes locked onto the bed, taking in the sight of the sleeping girl curled up against the pillows. Kursed laughed, "See? He has something in here. And it's a cute something, too."

Thane eyed her warily, "Kursed, this might be a trap. She might be one of them."

Kursed shook his head, "No. Impossible." He sniffed the air, "She smells....human. She could be an innocent."

Thane growled, "Whatever. You want her, take her and let's go!"

Kursed smiled, "Right." He scooped her up into his arms, looking over at Thane, "Let's go. I think Xanatos gets our point."

"Point?" Thane asked, "What point? I didn't see a point in this little raid."

Kursed laughed, "One, it'll tell him that we won't give up. And two, always expect the unexpected." He winked, "The window makes a good escape." He ran over to it, ready to jump, "Let's go, Thane. Can't just stand around."

"I'd rather just kill Xanatos and get that over with," Thane grumbled.

Kursed laughed, "Then I'd be out one partner." He gestured to Thane, "After you." Thane looked back at the door, before jumping out the window, Kursed following behind him. Thane growled, landing. Kursed was a handful, and no doubt, this girl would be, too. He smirked. At least Xanatos would be ticked. Thane let out a low laugh. Oh yeah, this was gonna be fun. They took off for the trees, hiding in the shadows.

Xanatos noticed two blurs running past him, running away. He smirked, two more cowards to hunt down and kill later. He looked back at the window. No one would stop him now. That girl was now his, and nothing could dampen his mood. He laughed, enjoying the fight, eager to get back to the girl.

Chapter2

Her head was throbbing. It felt like tiny hammers were going off in her head. Slowly, she opened her eyes, staring face to face with a small girl with scarlet red eyes. Her eyes widened. "Hey everybody!" She cried out, "I think she's awake!" Asuka cried out, eyes wide. The small girl jumped, clearly spooked.

She continued to scream, until a gentle hand placed itself on her shoulder. She whirled around, eyes wide, staring right into a set of mismatched eyes, one green, one purple. He smiled, "Relax, we're the good guys." A blonde snorted, looking away, "I heard that."

"Can somebody just please explain what's going on?" Asuka asked.

Silver-hair laughed, "Sure. What would you like to know?"

Asuka shrugged, "I don't know." She thought for a moment, "How did I get here?"

Blonde sighed, "My enthusiastic partner took you during a raid. Let's just say he wouldn't leave without you."

"Hey," Silver-hair growled, "She was gonna be his if we hadn't taken her."

"Alright!" Asuka exclaimed, holding up her hands, "Enough! Kinda starting to become the third-wheel here!"

The small girl smiled, "Maybe we should introduce ourselves."

Silver-hair laughed, "Good point."

The small girl nodded, jumping up and down, "Me first! Me first!"

Silver-hair smiled, "Of course, Lil, go ahead."

She nodded, looking over at Asuka. "Hi!" She exclaimed, "I'm Lilan!" A small dragon peeked out from over her shoulder, blue eyes curious. She giggled, "And this is Silver, my pet. He protects me, and is very sweet and loving. I'm a tomboy, obviously. I like to fight! I-!"

Silver-hair laughed, placing a hand on her shoulders, " Okay, Lil, that's enough."

She whirled on him, eyes now an icy blue while her hair turned silver, fangs and claws bared, "Let me finish!"

Silver-hair gave a nervous chuckle, "O-okay. Take it easy. Go ahead and finish."

She nodded, hair and eyes returning to normal. She smiled sweetly, "Thank you." She looked back at Asuka, "I love to read, anime is my favorite. I love any sport that relates to ice and snow, like ice skating. I'm a protective vampire. I also have a special gift. Wanna know what it is?"

Asuka gave her a nervous look, eyes wide. She chuckled nervously, "Heh, heh, sure."

She smiled slyly, "I have the gift of song."

Asuka's eyes narrowed in confusion, "What's that?"

Lilan came closer, "Whatever I sing, happens, and I do sing a lot." She smiled, "Also, it wouldn't be a good idea to tick me off. You saw what I almost did to him a few minutes ago." She giggled, "I also have a bro, but I barely see him. I'm also an orphan. Parents' were killed by others who wanted me."

Silver-hair sighed, "Are you quite finished, Lil?"

She nodded, "Yup!"

Asuka laughed, "Quite spunky for a seven year old, don't ya think?"

Lilan growled, "I'm twelve and a half!"

Asuka laughed, "My mistake, Lilan."

Lilan laughed, "Call me Lil! I'm sure we'll be great friends!"

Silver-hair laughed, "Who's next?"

Blonde sighed, looking over, "Thane. Pleasure."

14

Silver-hair laughed, placing an arm around his shoulders, "Now, Thane. Be nice. Tell this nice girl a little about yourself."

Thane growled, "Fine." He came close to her, dark grey eyes narrowed in amusement, while his voice became low, almost chilling, "Well, where to begin?" He laughed, sending shivers down her spine, "I'm a hybrid, half vampire, half wolf. Which means, yes, I will become a rather large wolf, so watch out. I used to kill for fun, and used to work for the enemy, Thankfully, I got out of it before I got in too deep." He laughed, "I can be dark, at times, and I control the shadows. Maybe I'll teach ya a few things, kid."

Asuka growled, "I'm eighteen, to let ya know!"

Thane let out a bark of a laugh, placing a hand under her chin and lifting her face up to meet his, "And feisty to boot." He looked over at Silver-hair, "I guess I told her everything"

Silver-hair laughed, "Better than nothing, I suppose." He got close to Asuka, eyes glinting with amusement, "And I'm Kursed. I'm a vampire. I love ramen, which Meagen makes, and is wonderful. I am very friendly, and very, very protective. I am currently working with the rebels, trying to bring peace. I can be serious at times." He smirked, coming close to her lips, "Now, what do you say about dating?"

Her eyes widened. Face red, she brought her hand back and smacked him across his face, hard. She growled, "What would make you think that?!"

Kursed laughed, "Guess I deserved that."

Lilan came up next to her, "What about you, lady? What's your name?"

Asuka smiled, "My name is Asuka." Her stomach growled, echoing throughout the room, "And...I'm hungry."

Thane growled, "I'm going to train."

"You're not gonna stick around?" Kursed asked, eyes wide.

Thane refused to look at him, "It's not my job to babysit a mere child." He left the room.

Kursed looked back at Asuka, "Shall we go to the kitchen?" She nodded. He held out his hand, "Follow me." She took it, feeling her head swim slightly. Lilan laughed, leading the way. Minutes later, they stepped off the last step and stopped in front of a slim door on their left. Lilan grabbed it, holding it open for Kursed and Asuka. He smiled, "After you."

Her eyes widened as she entered the room, taking in the sights. There were several pantries around the room, well stocked with food and spices. A large freezer door was on her right. Up against the wall in front of her was a large oven, pots boiling on the top. She sniffed, stomach growling loudly again, "Everything smells....so....good."

Kursed laughed, "I don't see Meagen here." He took a small ladle off the rack in front of him, "She won't know if I took a small taste of her ramen." He dipped the ladle in, then brought it up to his mouth, about to take a bite.

A small wooden spoon came down, smacking his hand. He cried out, dropping the ladle. He slowly looked over to see a pair of hazel green eyes narrowed in annoyance, "How many times do I have to tell you?! Don't take samples from my kitchen! Geez, Kursed! You're so stubborn!"

"Aww," He said, "But I just wanted a small bite."

"Wait," Asuka said, confused, "I thought vampires couldn't eat normal food? And if they did, it would be tasteless to them."

Kursed smirked, "A cliché. We can eat normal food from time to time." He laughed, "But I also need blood to survive."

The girl pushed him away, "Easy, Kursed." She looked over at Asuka, eyes narrowed, "And...who are you?"

Kursed placed a hand on her shoulder, "Now, Meagen, be nice. This is our new girl, Asuka. She's hungry. Wanna tell her a bit about yourself while fixing her something to eat?" She shot him a look, holding a large knife in her hands.

Asuka jumped up from the stool she was sitting on, "Here, I can take care of myself."

The girl shot her a look, growling, "Sit....back....down."

Asuka gave a nervous laugh, "Alright. Take it easy." She slowly inched back to her seat, sitting back down.

She sniffed, going back to the stove, "Now. The name's Meagen. I'm very independent, extremely strong, and can fight." She scooped out some ramen into a small bowl, placing it down in front of her, "Plus, I know secrets that can make your hair curl." She eyed Asuka, lip curling, "Not a pun. Now," She gestured to the bowl, "Now, eat. Eat. No one lets my food go to waste."

Asuka nodded, digging in. Slowly, she took a small, tentative bite. Her eyes closed, happy at last, "It's...so...good." She took another bite, then another, eyes now scrunched up, mouth full. She let out a few, muffled sounds before she swallowed, "But it's....too....hot!"

Meagen laughed, "Of course! That's because it's been on my stove." Kursed reached out again, trying to steal another bite. She smacked his hand away, growling, teeth clenched, "You can have it later."

Two young boys came in, eyes full of curiosity. One had black hair with silver streaks here and there, silver eyes were wide with amusement. The other had grey hair with black strands, yellow eyes narrowed, as if bored. Apart from those differences, they could have been twins. Black-hair laughed, "Meagen, is Kursed giving you trouble?"

Kursed let out a small whine, pouting, "Everybody's being mean to me today."

Black-hair laughed, "Someone has to be. Just wouldn't be the same." He reached out, snatching a piece of bread from around Meagen, laughing.

Meagen growled, "Can you wait for dinner?!"

Black-hair laughed, "Nope. Not really." He looked over at Asuka. "Hey," He whistled, "You're a pretty new face."

Asuka nodded, "I'm Asuka. It's nice to meet you."

Black-hair smiled, "I'm Cyrus. That's my bro, Cyro." He nodded to Grey-hair, tossing half of his bread to him. Grey-hair nodded, "He's a man of little words."

"Am not!" He exclaimed, "I'm Cyro. Charmed."

Cyrus laughed, "He's a little cold at times, but he'll warm up to you in no time." He smiled, "We're the Lycan twins, and we're very, very protective."

Kursed yawned, "Sorry to break up this crazy little group, but we've got others to introduce to Asuka." He took her by the hand, "Let's go."

Cyrus waved, "It was nice meeting you, Asuka!"

Kursed growled, "They can get on my nerves sometimes, I swear." He smiled, "Anyways, I should introduce you to our combat team. They also teach classes for the newbie's." He led the way through the dark hallway, finally getting to a rather large door. He smiled, opening it. He grunted, "It's heavy." He gestured forward, "After you." Asuka nodded, entering the large room.

She could barely see anything, thanks to the dim lighting. She squinted, "Is anyone here?"

A young woman stepped out from the shadows, hair more vibrant than Asuka's. Her red eyes glinted, "New girl, huh?" She giggled, "This'll be lovely."

Kursed stepped forward, smiling, "Why don't you introduce yourself, so she can get to know you?"

The woman smiled, red eyes glowing, "My name is Lynx. I'm a vampire, obviously. I am one of the hand-to-hand combat teachers. More than likely, I will be teaching you. I can control plants and fire, which can come in handy from time to time." Her eyes narrowed in puzzlement, "Where's Deacon?"

A figure came out of the shadows, frost blue eyes glinted, "Here, Lynx." He smiled, moving small strands of hair out of his face, "What's up?"

She nodded toward Asuka, "Dear, this lovely young girl is Asuka. Say hello, dear."

He nodded, "Yo! My name's Deacon. I'm a vampire, of course. But I have an unusual ability. Wanna hear it?"

She nodded, "Sure. If you want to tell me."

He smiled, "I can enter others dreams and attack from there. Maybe I'll teach ya sometime. I am also the other hand-to-hand combat teachers, and most likely be teaching you alongside Lynx, here." He laughed, "Where's Kershaw?"

"Good question," Lynx said, "Kershaw! Get out here! We have a new student!"

Out from the shadows stepped a young boy with silver hair, and icy blue eyes, a small smile on his lips, "Yes Lynx? What did you need?"

She gestured to Asuka, "Say hi, Kershaw."

He held out his hand, "I'm Kershaw. Nice to meet you!"

Asuka smiled, "Likewise."

He smiled, "I'm a lycan. I also teach the stealth classes. You'll be in mine, along with Kursed."

Kursed sighed, "For the fifth time."

Kershaw laughed, "Where's Lilan?"

Kursed smiled, "Must have stayed behind with Meagen. She does like to help out in the kitchen, after all."

Kershaw nodded, "That's Lil for ya!" He narrowed his eyes, "Where's Klax?"

Kursed rolled his eyes, "Beats me. Isn't he in here?" He growled, "Klax? You here?"

Another figure stepped out from the shadows, chainmail clanking as he walked. He stepped into the light, forest green eyes narrowed, looking at Asuka, "Yes?"

Kursed gestured to Asuka, "Meet the new girl! Asuka!"

Asuka smiled, blushing slightly, "Hello."

He gave her a blank look, "I'm Klax. I teach the weapons class here. I'll teach you how to fight with different weapons. Hopefully, starting soon."

She nodded, "I hope I can get to know each and every one of you."

The door opened, making them all jump. They looked around, trying to see. Thane stood there, eyes narrowed, "Asuka. You're to come with me. Our queen would like to speak with you." She gulped, the fear creeping back into her heart, making her shake. He held out his hand, "Let's go."

***Xx

Xanatos growled, reentering the room where he last left Asuka. Hopefully now, she would be awake. He laughed, "Now, my dear, where were we?" He cut off, seeing an empty bed. He closed his eyes, growling. Raising his fist, he slammed it into a wall, leaving cracks where his fist was. "Ivory!" He cried out.

Out from the shadows stepped a young girl, crimson eyes narrowed in amusement, while her belts and buckles jangled as she walked, "Yes, Xanatos?"

He growled, eyes blazing, "Go out, and bring back the girl who was in this room. Her name is Asuka. Don't harm her. Kill anyone who gets in your way."

She nodded, "With pleasure." Her eyes glinted as she laughed, an eerie bone chilling sound, "I'll have her here soon."

Chapter 3

A figure ran through the shadows, nose twitching every few minutes. Ivory smirked, crimson eyes twinkling
g in amusement, "I've got your scent, little one." She giggled, "I'm getting closer." She laughed, continuing to run.

***

Asuka continued to shake, keeping her eyes low to the ground. Thane cast a curious glance over at her, holding back a smile. "Scared?" He taunted.

She quickly shook her head, "N-no, no. I'm not scared."

He looked over at her, seeing her blush, "You're blushing."

Her eyes widened, "I am not!" She ran forward, trying to escape his gaze. *Why?* She thought, *why does he stare at me with those eyes? Eyes that are almost always hiding something.* He growled, racing after her, finally gripping her arm in an iron grip.

He locked eyes with her, steely grey meeting emerald green, smiling, "You really are a feisty one."

She pulled away, eyes narrowed, "Can we just go? I'd rather just get this over with." She tried to take several deep, even breaths.

Ugh! She thought, *Why does he have to be so irritating'*

He sighed, rubbing his head, this girl was too stubborn. He walked ahead, leading the way. Minutes later, they stopped at a large door. Thane gripped the heavy handle and pulled it, opening to reveal a dark room. He gestured forward, "After you." She nodded shakily, eyes wide.

She stepped forward, the dark beginning to strain her eyes. "Hello?" She called out, wary. Her eyes began to adjust. The room was huge, filled with hanging draperies around a silver throne. Pillows were scattered everywhere, acting as extra seats. In the center if the silver throne sat a young, pale woman, silver eyes narrowed as she listened to a young boy.

Hearing the sounds of footsteps, she looked up, smirking, "Thane, dear, hello?"

He bowed in front of her, "My Queen, as requested, I've brought her here." His eyes narrowed in puzzlement, "Who is this?"

The boy looked over at him, amethyst eyes wide, "Hello! I'm Lunarias!" He looked around Thane to get a better look at Asuka. He whistled, smoothing back a few strands of silver hair from his face. He gently took her hand, "Well, hello there." He kissed her hand, "And who might you be?"

Asuka blushed, eyes wide, "A-Asuka."

He smiled, "I'm new around these parts myself. How'd you like sticking with me?"

Thane growled, putting both hands on her shoulders, "She's mine."

Lunarias gave a nervous laugh, placing both hands into the air, "Okay, okay, big guy. She's yours. I got it." He narrowed his eyes, curling his lip and growling.

The woman clapped her hands, "Enough. Take it outside boys." She looked over at Asuka, smiling gently, "Come closer, child. I won't harm you." Asuka stepped forward, trying to keep her breathing even. The woman smiled, voice smooth as silk, "Tell me, child, what is your name?"

"Asuka, your majesty," She said, uneasy.

The woman laughed, tossing her long black hair back, "It's lovely to meet you, Asuka." She cleared her throat, "My name is Lilth, Queen of the rebels. And," She smiled, "Your boss."

Asuka's eyes widened, "Y-You're our boss?"

Lilth laughed, a pretty tinkling sound, "Surprised?"

Asuka nodded quickly, "Y-Yes! Uh, I mean no, your majesty."

Lilth smiled, "Well, what did you expect? Some old geezer?"

Asuka blushed again, "N-no, no, I didn't. Honest."

Lilth bowed her head, "It's alright. I didn't really want anyone to know, because I had a feeling I would get almost the same reaction as I did from you. Or worse."

"Worse?" Asuka asked, eyes wide.

Thane butt in, cutting them both off, "Lilth, what did you need to see her for?"

She blinked in surprise. "Oh!" She said, "Asuka, do you still have that camera from your recon mission I gave you?"

Asuka nodded, pulling it out of her pocket. "Here," She placed it into her outstretched hand, I almost didn't get out of there alive." She narrowed her eyes, "Wait. Where am I, anyway?"

"To answer your question, this is a training school for new recruits, and our little hideaway," Lilth nodded, "As for taking you, it seemed both Kursed and Thane took a liking to you."

Thane snarled, "I….I don't l-l-like her!"

Asuka made a face, "Ugh! I don't like him! I was forcibly taken!"

Lilth narrowed her eyes, "Nevertheless, you both took her. Thane, you and Kursed are now linked with this girl. Protect her."

Thane narrowed his eyes, sighing, "Fine." He started to leave, "Let's go, brat."

Asuka growled, "Brat?!" She ran after him, "Say that again!"

Lilth laughed, "I think that girl will change both Kursed and Thane. And it will be for the better." A shadow fell upon her, making her look around. She locked eyes with a shadowy figure, hunched over. Her eyes grew wide, "Who are you?"

A young woman with bleached-blonde hair looked up at her, holding onto two unconscious girls. Her red eyes were narrowed. Slowly, she se the two girls down, placing a hand on top of each of their heads. "Please!" She rasped, "Help us. You're the only one who can!"

Lilth looked at each of the girls. One had long, silky black hair, wearing a purple skirt and black halter, a slim purple choker hanging loosely around her neck. The other had short, dark purple hair, wearing a ripped, purple dress. Lilth's eyes widened to the size of quarters. She knelt down beside her, "Tell me everything that happened. But first, your name."

The womans' eyes hardened, "Samantha Grimm."

***

Asuka chased after Thane, growing more and more annoyed, "Get back here!" A small blur rushed past Thane, crashing hard right into Asuka. She let out a small whoosh of air, falling backwards.

Lilan squealed, "Asuka! How did it go?"

A boy stepped out from the shadows, blue eyes narrowed under his silver bangs, "Lilan, go easy on the mortal."

Lilan giggled, "Sorry, Silver."

"Silver?!" Asuka exclaimed, "No way!"

Lilan looked over at Silver, "Forgot to tell ya, he can turn into a human at will. Comes in handy here and there." She looked up at Thane, eyes narrowed, "He didn't do anything….vulgar to you, did he?"

Thane turned red, eyes wide. He shook his head wildly, "N-no! Don't be vulgar!"

Asuka looked up at Lilan, still kneeling on the floor, " Hey, do you know where I can get a change of clothes? I kinda need to change."

Lilan pulled her up, giggling, "Of course! I'll show ya!" She pulled her along the hallway, laughing all the way. Thane was about to follow, when a black blur raced past them, running right into the throne room.

Thane stared after the blur in puzzlement, "What was that about?" He ran forward, "Lilan! Take care of Asuka! I'll go see what's going on!" He left them behind.

Lilan narrowed her eyes, "O…kay." She looked up at Asuka, "Let's go get you some new clothes!" They took off down the hall, racing the shadows.

Thane burst into the throne room, eyes narrowed. Three girls were on the ground, breathing hard. Lilth looked at the girl, eyes wide while kneeling beside her, "Tell me everything that happened. But first, your name."

The blonde narrowed her eyes, "Samantha Grimm."

***

The shadowy figure came skidding to a stop, breathing hard. Ivory smiled, fangs glinting, "I've found you, little one." She laughed, "I can't wait to bring you back. And." She studied her claws for a second, "To kill anyone who tries to get in my way." She giggled, relishing the anticipation for the kill.

Chapter 4

Lilan giggled as she opened the door, "In here, Asuka!" She ran inside, beckoning to her, "Come on! Come on! Hurry up!"

Asuka laughed, "Okay, okay. Calm down, I'm coming." She ducked inside, eyes filled with excitement. The minute she stepped inside, her eyes widened. "Wow," She whistled, "This room is *huge*!" The room was circular, with a huge window, looking out to a medium balcony. Around the room hung little, soft lights, twinkling cheerfully.

Lilan smiled, "Do you like it?"

Asuka nodded quickly, "Like it? I love it!" She grinned wildly, "It's wonderful!" She sent Lilan a quick, curious look, "Lil, why are you showing me this room?"

Lilan laughed, "Lilth said you could stay, right?" Asuka nodded, "Well, I figured you should get your own room!"

Asuka looked over at her, eyes wide, "Y-you mean….this is *my room*?" She giggled, running over and jumping onto the bed, pillows rising slightly into the air. She laughed, "This….is so….*cool*!"

Lilan winked, "Wait 'til you see your clothes!" She threw open the doors, revealing several dresses, along with combat garb. Lilan laughed, watching Asuka step closer, "These are all yours!"

Asuka reached out, feeling the material on one. She whistled,

"This….this is impressive. And probably expensive."

Lilan shook her head, "Nope! Lilth made sure we were all cared for." She smiled, "She may seem cold at first, but that's how she shows her kindness. She just wants you to feel as comfortable as possible."

Asuka pulled off a dark, forest green dress, eyes curious. A small smile graced her lips, "I like this one." She narrowed her eyes, "But I think it could use some adjustments." She looked over at Lilan, "Got any scissors? Hmmm…and belts?"

Lilan smiled slyly, "I'll see what we've got around here. Hand on, lemme go check." She went to turn around, then froze, "Thane?"

Thane stood in the doorway, eyes narrowed in amusement, "Playing dress-up, are we?"

Asuka growled, "What do you want?"

"Relax, princess," He spat, "It has nothing to do with you." He looked over at Lilan, "Lil, Lilth wants to see you. Something about several newcomers, and extra rooms."

Lilan's eyes widened in excitement, "Of course!" She ran over to him. Quickly, she looked back, "Looks like you'll have to wait, Asuka. I'll be back soon!" She waved as they walked away.

Asuka sighed, looking back at the dress. A slim shadow fell over her, reaching over her shoulders. "Hey, Asuka," A male voice chuckled, holding a slinky, black, revealing number, "Why don't you wear this one for me, hmm?"

She turned around, eyes wide, "Kursed!" She smacked his shoulder, "Very funny!" She looked away, "What to do you want?"

"Besides you?" He chuckled, "Nothing, just wandering around. I wanted to see you."

She sighed, "Kursed, can you let me dress in peace?" She cast daggers at him, "Please?"

He laughed, "Alright, take it easy. I'll go wait out in the hall," He chuckled to himself, leaving the room.

She sighed in relief, "Finally." Quickly, she slipped into the green dress, stepping out of her black garb in the process. She smiled, twirling around a few times as the skirt flowed around her ankles. "Alright, Kursed," She called out, "You can come back in, now." No answer, "Kursed?" She jumped as she heard small, quick footsteps. She rolled her eyes, "Kursed, if this is some stupid way to scare me, I swear I'll-!" She turned around, breaking off in mid sentence, seeing a young woman with bright, crimson red eyes. The woman smiled, backhanding her across the face. Asuka cried out, slamming backwards into the wall, finally sliding down. She shook her head, "Ugh, felt like I got hit with a metal pipe." She looked up, seeing the woman advance. Her entire body shook, eyes wide, "W-who are you?"

Her cold, icy hand wrapped tightly around her throat, lifting her off of the ground. Asuka tried to speak, tried to force air into her lungs, but the woman tightened her grip, smiling, "So, you're the one Xanatos wanted, hmmm?" She giggled, "I know he said don't harm you. But I don't think he'll mind if I left you in pieces." She growled, "Let's play!" She threw Asuka to the opposite wall, grinning as she heard Asuka's head smack hard into the wall.

Asuka groaned, seeing stars. She slowly raised her head up, *I can't fight her! If I try, I'd be killed! Man, she hits hard, though. Harder than I've ever felt.*

Asuka coughed weakly, "Please....don't."

The woman growled, grasping her wrist in her hands, "Hush, now. Everything will be alright." She bared her fangs, laughing, "I think Xanatos won't mind if I went first, first, no?" She raised her hand up, quickly sinking her fangs in deep. Asuka cried out, trying to struggle, but the woman held on tight, growling. Asuka felt her vision start to blur, the room spinning.

Asuka groaned, "Someone...anyone...help." Her hand fell, mind growing fuzzy, then black.

The woman let go, letting her hand drop to the ground. She slowly licked her lips, eyes filled with pure insanity. She looked back at Asuka, who was struggling to keep her eyes open. She lifted the small girl easily off of the ground, throwing her over her shoulder. She sighed, "Let's go." She turned around, staring face to face with Thane.

Thane growled, eyes narrowed, "Let....her....go."

Ivory hissed softly, "She's my prey." She grinned, "I see why he wants her now, too." She looked back at him, "You won't be able to stop me."

Thane growled, eyes growing darker, "I'll ask you politely, one more time, let her go."

She snarled, letting her body drop to the ground. She beckoned forward, eyes filled with malice, "Bring it!" She leapt forward, claws aimed for his face. Thane gripped her wrist, falling backwards. Bringing his foot up, he kicked her hard, kicking her halfway to the other wall. She slid down, breathing hard, "Kid, you're stronger than….I thought. Tell me, you're more than a vampire, aren't you?"

Thane laughed, voice almost inhuman, "Wouldn't you like to know?" His body began to blur, before finally vanishing, able to walk freely around her, "Tell me, young one, what's your name?"

"You're taunting me," She hissed, crimson eyes narrowed, "Why do you want to know my name?"

She cried out as something jabbed right into her back, making her sprawl out onto the ground. Thane laughed, reappearing behind her, knee pinning her down while pulling her head back, "Because I want to know the name of who I'm killing."

She let out a chuckle, "You've got guts, mutt, I'll give you that." She narrowed her eyes, "Ivory."

"Huh?" Thane asked, confused.

"My name," She growled, "My name is Ivory."

"Ivory, huh?" He chuckled to himself, "Pretty name."

"Not as pretty as Asuka, right?" She laughed, "You don't have to answer that. But don't I get to at least know yours?"

"Why should you know mine?" He asked.

She sent him a look, "Because I want to know who it is I get to kill next time." She chuckled, vanishing into the floor. Thane's eyes widened, trying to grab her, but missed. He growled, pounding his fist into the ground.

"Thane?" A voice said, making him look up. His eyes widened even more.

Kursed stood at the door, unsure if he could run in. He ran in anyway, dropping down to where Asuka lay, unconscious. His nose twitched, "Thane, what happened?" He went to roll her over, see if she was hurt anywhere. Kursed lifted up her hand, eyes widening in shock,

"Thane." He showed him her hand, where Ivory got to her. His nose twitched, fangs bared. He paused, slowly moving his hands away, eyes widening. He slowly got up, taking a few steps back, "I'm sorry." He took a few more steps back, "I have to go!" He ran out of the room, hiding his face.

Thane watched him leave, before looking back at Asuka. His eyes narrowed in confusion, looking at the small wound on her hand, "What is it about you that made him leave? What did Ivory mean, by 'why he wanted you'?" He sighed, picking her up off the floor and laying her gently onto the bed. He carefully moved a few strands of hair from her face, sighing, "What am I going to do with you?" He walked over to the door, "Should go get you something for your hand." He looked down, "Sorry I couldn't get here sooner." He walked away, letting her sleep. He chuckled to himself, "You're more trouble than you're worth, you know that?" He continued down the dark hallway, moving quickly out of sight.

Chapter 5

Kursed ran down the hall, head bowed. *Ugh,* He thought, *What was wrong with me? I....All I did was catch that scent and...*His eyes widened, *That's it! That's what set me off!* He growled, *Need to ask Lilan about it when I can.*

He turned the corner and entered the kitchen, quickly shutting the door. He sighed, looking up at Meagen, who was giving him a weird look, "Oh! Hello, there, Meagen. Nice to see you again!"

Meagen narrowed her eyes, "Something wrong, Kursed?"

He growled, "Don't get me started." He walked over to the pantry, and pulled out a small, slim bottle, a dark liquid sticking to the sides. He quickly pulled off the top and took a swig.

She giggled, "Something happen?"

He gave her a look, "Sure, let's go with that." He took another swig.

Meagen came up to him, placing a small hand on his shoulder. "Kursed," Her eyes were wide, "Please, if something's wrong, tell me. I'd be happy to help."

He started to open his mouth, about to speak, when the door was thrust open. A figure stood there, eyes narrowed. "Kursed!" Cyrus said, "Lilth needs both you and Meagen to come to the meeting room, now."

Meagen narrowed her eyes, "And if I refuse?"

Cyrus shrugged, "I don't know. She just asked for everyone to be there." He took off, racing down the hall.

Kursed looked down at Meagen, smiling slightly, "We'd better go. I don't feel like angering Lilth."

She blushed, "Right." She quickly pulled her hand away, "Sorry." But he was already out of the room. She sighed, eyes downcast, "Kursed, I wish you could see." She shook her head, before running after him.

***

"Here, Thane," Lilan said, handing him the small bowl.

He looked up at her and smiled slightly, "Thanks." He said, getting close to Asuka, "Keep the cold cloth nearby. This is gonna hurt her." He raised her hand up, "Keep her still."

She nodded, "Right." She placed two small, pale hands on her shoulders, nodding still.

He lifted her hand to his face and gently placed his lips over her wound, eyes closed. Asuka moaned, shifting slightly. She moaned, scrunching up her face in pain. "Ugh," She cried out, "No….stop it." She cried out, tensing up.

Lilan gently held her down, tears forming in her eyes, "Asuka, please. You need to calm down. This will only hurt for a second. Please, Asuka."

Thane let go of her hand, spitting out the poisoned blood into the small bowl. He sighed, "Thank the Moon. A small amount of poison got into her blood." He looked up at Lilan, smiling, "Don't look so sad. She's gonna be okay." He growled, tearing off a strip of cloth with his teeth, pressing it down to stop the bleeding. She moaned, tensing up again, "Ugh, Th…ane." She let out a small breath, before relaxing.

He looked down at Asuka, moving hair from her face. Quickly, he dipped another small piece of cloth into another small bowl of water, and dabbing it on her cut. "Now," He mumbled, "Where did I put that ointment?"

Lilan looked around, reaching over to his side and grasping it. She handed it up to him, "Here, Thane. I think this is what you're looking for."

Thane looked up from his search, smiling, "Oh. Thank you, Lilan." He took the tube from her hands, placing a small dab on the wound. Asuka hissed, eyes scrunched up in pain again, before relaxing, hand going limp. He sighed, wrapping up her hand. "There," he smiled, "All better now." He looked up, seeing Lilan's head bowed. "Lil," He said voice soft, "What's wrong?"

She looked up at him, blood red tears running down her cheeks. Her shoulders shook, "I…only left her for….a few seconds…and she…got attacked." She wiped her tears away, smiling slightly, "But…she wouldn't want me to cry." She sniffled, "She's so sweet. Kinda like a mother to me."

Thane looked back down at Asuka, who was now sleeping peacefully. He smiled, reaching over and ruffling Lilan's head. "You're a good kid," He said, "You just need the right nudge, now and again." He looked up, hearing several footsteps run past her door. Growling, he leapt up from the bed, sprinting over to the door, "Cyrus!"

The young boy skidded slightly, eyes wide, "Thane! Thank God I've found you. Lilth has summoned all of us. Those two girls have finally awoken."

"Huh?" He asked, "Which two girls?"

"Just come and see," Cyrus said, "I've got to go!" He turned and continued running down the hall.

Thane growled, eyes narrowed, "Now what was that about?"

Lilan came up to him, grabbing his arm, "C'mon. We'd better go see." She pulled him along, "I'd hate to tick off Lilth."

He looked down at her, nodding. "Right," He laughed, "She's scary when she's upset." They laughed, running down the hall.

 ***

Lilth sighed, hearing the door open again. She rolled her eyes, looking over at Thane and Lilan, "You're late."

Thane bowed, starting to open his mouth to speak, when Lilan jumped up, smiling, "We're not late. We're just early, is all."

Thane gave a nervous chuckle, "Sorry, your highness." He stood up straight, "We were busy taking care of Asuka."

Lilth smiled, "Of course." She bowed her head, "I hope she feels better." She looked up, "Now that you're here, we can get started." She gestured over to the three young girls standing in the shadows, gesturing, "Girls, you may begin."

The blonde nodded, "Pleasure. My name is Samantha Grimm. And I escaped from Xanatos's stronghold with these two girls."

Lilth nodded, "Yes, you mentioned that. Tell us a bit about yourself."

Samantha nodded, "As you wish." She cleared her throat, "I used to be part of the AoDA in my city, which stands for Angel of Death Academy. Unfortunately, I lost my angel wings during a fight, where they were painfully ripped off, thanks to a rouge hybrid. After a mishap with my brother at the academy, I resigned. Wandering the city, I was attacked by a vampire. Now, normally, I don't really explain my past to anyone, but I had to tell Lilth, otherwise, I would have been thrown out." She smiled, "So, looks like I'm stuck here for awhile."

Lilth nodded, "Glad to have you with us, Miss Samantha."

"Please," She held up a hand, "Call me Sam."

Lilth smiled, "Of course." She turned to the smaller girls, "Ladies, you're next."

The one with deep, violet hair smiled, "My name is Cloe." She smiled, "I'm a hybrid, one of the rarest breeds." Her face grew serious, "I was taken from Xanatos's stronghold." She tugged at the small collar around her neck, a broken chain dangling, swinging from side to side, "Sadly, I was a slave for him."

Lilan's eyes went wide. She quickly ran to her, throwing her in a tight embrace, "Oh, I'm so, so sorry."

Cloe laughed, "What are you sorry about?"

Lilan looked up at her, smiling softly, "Well, I kinda know how you feel." She pulled away, "I think we'll be great friends."

Cloe smiled, violet eyes twinkling, "Of course!" She laughed, "I'd like that!"

The one in all black spoke up next, voice soft, almost quiet, "Hello. I'm Sofy." She bowed her head, tugging at a similar collar around her neck, silver chain dangling, "As you can see, I too, was a slave." She beamed at them, "I am a quiet girl, and I tend to keep to myself from time to time. But I am very friendly, and am always willing to help where I can." She bowed, "Thank you for accepting us."

Lilth smiled, "Not at all. It's a pleasure, gaining new recruits." She gestured to everyone, "Please, step forward and introduce yourselves to them, make them feel welcome."

Thane stepped forward first, "Thane, pleasure."

Lilan smiled, bouncing around, "Lilan! Call me Lil." Silver poked his head from over her shoulder, "This is Silver, my pet. He's pleased to meet you, too."

Kursed smirked, "Kursed. I'm sure we'll get along just fine."

Meagen smiled, waving, "Hey, I'm Meagen. Nice to meet you!"

Lunarias looked at them, saluting, "Lunarias. How do?"

Cyrus and Cyro stepped forward, bouncing on the balls of their feet. Cyrus smiled, "I'm Cyrus, and this is my twin brother, Cyro."

Cyro nodded, "Pleasure."

Deacon and Lynx stepped forward, smiling. Deacon bowed his head, "I'm Deacon, and this is my mate, Lynx."

She smiled, "We'll try to make you feel right at home."

Kershaw waved, "Name's Kershaw. What's up?"

Klax sent them a look, "I'm Klax. Charmed."

Lilth smiled, "Thank you for those lovely intros." She grew serious, "Listen, so far, our little human doesn't know about the *rehabilitation* we do here for those under Xanatos's control. Let's keep it that way. For if she was to stumble upon that area, she'd more than likely be killed. Am I clear?" They nodded, eyes narrowed. "Now," She said, "Please, go back to your duties. But please, treat our guests with respect, and make them feel right at home." She bowed, before turning to leave, skirts swishing in the shadows. Her eyes glinted as a small smile painted itself upon her lips.

Thane sighed, looking over at Kursed. "Hey," He looked over at Thane, "Asuka's alright. You should visit her soon." He turned to leave.

Kursed bowed his head, looking at his clawed hands. "Yeah," He whispered, voice low and hoarse, "Sure."

Chapter 6

Ivory growled, raking her claws against the stony wall. "Stupid brats!" She spat, "Why did they have to get in my way?!" She narrowed her crimson eyes, "As much as I hate to admit it, her blood was delicious, free of any impurities." She smirked, "I could probably take her and kill her myself." She laughed, "Only after I....*play* with her, first, break my new toy in." There was a loud, mournful howl, echoing all over the building, making Ivory shiver. She smirked, "And I think I know who can help me." Quick as a cat, she slithered through the shadows, eyes glowing.

Another loud howl, this time, closer. She giggled. "I'm getting closer," She said in a sing-song voice. She leapt out of the shadows, standing in front of a large, reinforced door. She quickly opened it, and stepped inside, shutting it behind her. She laughed, "Anyone home?" She reached over, flicking on a switch.

Around her were many different devices, ranging in size and shape, almost looking evil. In the center of the room, though, around the chains and cages, was a young woman in chains. Her silver hair was long and flat, hanging over her face like a curtain. Her eyes were closed, as if asleep. Her clothes looked ratty and torn, almost hanging off of her. She looked up at Ivory, snarling, "You here to try and '*rehabilitate*' me?" She chuckled, low and soft, "Forget it. You can never change me."

Ivory smiled, "Don't worry your pretty little head about that." She knelt down, staring right into her golden eyes, "Listen to me. I've got an offer for you. One that will set you free."

The woman smiled at her, eyes glinting, "Go on."

Ivory laughed, "Good girl. Now," She grew serious, "I'll set you free, if, and only if, you can do me a teensy, tiny favor."

The girl growled, "What do you need?"

Ivory narrowed her eyes, "I need to grab a target, and you're the only one who can help me."

She growled, "And if I refuse?"

Ivory shrugged, a sarcastic smile on her lips, "Then I guess you're stuck here, aren't you?"

She sighed, "What do I have to do?"

Ivory smiled again, "All you have to do is kill anyone who gets in my way. But you leave the girl to me."

She snorted, "So, what does this girl look like?"

Ivory thought for a moment, until, "Well, her hair is like the color of blood, while her eyes sparkle like emeralds." She winked, "But she's such a wuss when it comes to fighting, or being attacked." She narrowed her eyes, "There is one, though, I want you to save for me."

The woman chuckled, "Who's the lucky one?"

Ivory laughed, "Thing is, I don't really know his name." She grinned, "But he's simply delicious." She got up, "So, do we have a deal?"

The woman smiled, eyes full of amusement, "Sure. Why not? I've got nothing better to do as is."

Ivory smiled, "Atta girl!" She looked around, "Now, where's the key?"

The woman shook her head, "There is none. The chains are linked to the floor. Pressing the switch on the wall releases them."

Ivory smirked, "As long as you remain true to your word, and help me." She narrowed her eyes, "What's your name, anyhow?"

"Aurana," The woman said.

"Lovely, I'm Ivory," She searched the wall, "Hmmm…switch, switch. Where's the switch? Oh!" She clapped her hands, "Here it is!" She quickly pressed the button, cackling.

The chains clattered loudly to the floor, releasing her. Aurana laughed, "Oh, that feels good!"

Ivory narrowed her eyes, "Bring the girl here, and you can handle the rest."

Aurana grinned, "With pleasure." She laughed, eyes glowing in the dim light.

***

Asuka moaned, slowly opening her eyes, "Huh? What happened?" She flexed her hands, wincing as she did so. She looked down at her hand, noticing the makeshift bandage, "Oh yeah. Almost forgot about that." She slowly sat up, feeling a bit weak, "Ugh, she must have taken more out of me than I thought." She groaned, rolling out of bed, "Hello?" No answer, "Guys? Anyone?" She rolled her eyes, "Gotta go find them, I guess." She sighed.

She got up, feeling her knees grow weak. She let out a breath, "Guys, where are you?" Slowly and carefully, she made her way out of the room, taking a deep, shaky breath, narrowing her eyes, "Where could they be?" She started down the long, dark hallway.

Minutes later, she heard loud, mournful howling. She jumped, surprised, "What was that?!" She narrowed her eyes, listening. Quietly, she followed the howls, turning the corner and stopping right in front of a reinforced door. She frowned, listening again. Another howl, long and drawn out. Taking a deep breath, she raised a hand out, about to open the door.

She gasped, pulling her hand back, while shaking her head, "No, I can't. I don't even know what's in there."

Soft laughter made her jump, looking quickly around. Two, gentle hands placed themselves on her shoulders, goading her, "Go on. Open the door. You want to see the inside, yes?"

She shook her head, "It wouldn't be right."

The voice chuckled, "Go on. It's alright. Open it."

She closed her eyes, "Fine. Maybe I will." She took a deep breath, quickly opening her door, and peering inside, "Hello?"

There was barely a sound at first, until someone cackled, "Hello, child." The figure rushed forward, claws exposed. Asuka shrieked as a large, silver wolf pounces, landing on top of her. She grunted, trying to hold the beasts' jaws at bay.

She cried out, "Help! Someone, help me!"

***

Thane sighed, wandering the halls. Taking the time he had, he thought back to Asuka, lamenting. Oh, how he had wanted to betray himself, and rip out the young girls' throat, driving himself into a frenzy. But no, he had made a promise to Lilth, and to himself, to never harm a innocent again. Not after what happened last time. He shook his head, shrugging it off.

He turned the corner, lost in his thoughts, when he bumped into someone. He groaned, rubbing his nose, "Ugh, what hit me?" He shook his head, "You!"

Lunarias gave him a look, eyes cold, "Yeah, so?"

Thane snarled, "What do you want?"

Lunarias gave him a look, "I only want to talk. Is that alright with you?" Thane didn't answer, "Look, can we walk?" Thane nodded, "Good." They started down the hall, silent for awhile.

Lunarias broke the silence first, "So, what do you think of Asuka?"

Thane's face turned slightly red, eyes wide, "I....I have no idea what you're talking about."

Lunarias smiled, "I think you know." He shrugged, "I just want to know your input, is all."

Thane looked at him, eyes narrowed, "I feel nothing for her. She's just some weak mortal, who jumps at the smallest things."

Lunarias laughed, "Good. I'll make her mine, then."

Thane growled, "Stay...away...from...her." He walked on, leaving him behind.

Lunarias sighed, catching up to him, "I'm not finished yet!" He growled, "Are you always like this?"

"Like what?" He asked.

"You know," Lunarias said, "Cold, silent. Don't you ever talk to anyone?"

Thane shrugged, "Not really."

"Unless you're with Asuka," Lunarias teased. Thane spun around, claws unsheathed and about to slice into his face, when a loud scream pierced the silence, making them both jump in surprise. Lunarias stared off into the shadows, "What was that?"

"I don't know," Thane said, "But I'm going to find out!" He ran forward, following the screams. Rounding the corner, he saw Asuka wrestling with a large, silver beast, and loosing by the looks of it. Lunarias skidded up behind him.

She looked up at them, eyes narrowed, "About time!" She cried out, holding the wolf back, "Don't just stand there! Help me!"

Thane and Lunarias nodded, rushing forward. A small, lithe figure rushed out of the shadows, cackling, "Oh no, you don't!" Her claws reached out toward them, "You're my toys! Play with me instead!" They cried out, slamming hard into the wall.

Thane growled, "Ivory. How nice to see you again."

She laughed, "Still haven't told me your name."

"Thane," He said curtly.

She laughed, "Yay! My toy has a name!" She looked over at Lunarias, lip curling, "And….what's my other toys' name?"

"Lunarias," He croaked out, her hand slowly tightening around his throat.

She laughed, "New toys! Yay! And they finally have names!" She growled, "Let's play!" She lifted them up throwing them against the wall again, "Come on, play!"

Asuka grunted, "Ugh, get off me, fuzz-face!" She closed her eyes, "I said…get…off!"

Another fuzzy shape came flying out of the shadows, slamming hard into the wolf. Asuka looked around, eyes wide, "No!"

The silver wolf snarled, blue eyes narrowed, baring his teeth. They started circling each other, taking small nips of their fur here and there. The larger of the two lashed out, scratching blue-eyes' muzzle. He cried out, shaking his head. The larger wolf then leapt forward, sinking her teeth deep in the small ones' throat. He cried out, whimpering, while the other growled in victory. Asuka cried out as the large one let go, howling in triumph. Her eyes grew with shock, "No!" Horrified, she looked back at Thane and Lunarias, hoping they were having better luck, "Kershaw!"

They weren't. Ivory had her sights set on Lunarias, while Thane was left behind. He looked at Asuka, shielding her, "Asuka! Stay near me!" She felt his arms pull her in close, protecting her.

Lunarias chuckled, feeling Ivory's claws slice deep into his cheek. His eyes twinkled in amusement, "That's the best you got, hag?"

"*Hag?!*" She screeched in anger, gripping his shoulders, "You'll pay for that!" He brought up his knee, kneeing her hard in her stomach. She grunted, letting go.

He laughed, "What's that about payback?"

She smirked, "Just wait!" She rushed forward, too quickly for the eyes to see. Quickly, she jumped on top of him, growling, "Told you, you'd pay!" She growled, baring her fangs, before sinking them deep into his shoulder, making him cry out in pain. Slowly, his knees gave out, dropping his body to the floor, eyes closed in pain.

Ivory let go, letting his head drop. She smirked, "Aww....my toy broke." She looked over at the large wolf, "Awwww...yours broke, too." Hurried footsteps made her look around, "Wonderful. Best get out, before we're next! Aurana, move your tail!" The silver wolf nodded, following after her into the shadows.

Asuka tried to look over at Lunarias, but Thane blocked her view, shaking his head, "No, Asuka. Trust me, you don't want to see." He rested his face on top of her head, breathing deep, "I'm just glad you're okay."

She let out a loud sob, burrowing her face into his shoulder, "Thane, I was so scared."

"I know," he whispered, "I know."

***

Xanatos laughed, sitting in a darkened room, candles flickering everywhere, "So, Ivory, you've returned empty-handed, I see."

She bowed her head, "Forgive me, master. She had strong, powerful toys. I did manage to break one, though." She admired the room, seeing a small fountain in the one corner, trickling quietly. In the center, was a small blanket, giving anyone who walked in a relaxing place to sit. Ivory smiled, "Someone did manage to help me, though, breaking another toy in the process." She turned to the shadows, "Come on out, Aurana."

She came out of the shadows, yellow eyes glinting, "Hello, Xanatos. Lovely to see you again."

Ivory's jaw dropped, eyes wide, "What?! You two know each other?!"

Aurana nodded, "He offered me a mission to capture a girl, and infiltrate the enemy base. Unfortunately, I was stopped by the enemy, locked up, and forced to go through rehabilitation." She smirked, "But it was well worth it. I got some good information for you."

Xanatos got up from the ground, "Yes, I remember now." He chuckled, "Ivory, I sent her a long time ago, when I first heard about Asuka, of course. Asuka had just started training, though, and wasn't ready yet to go through the change." He smirked, "Ivory, I'd like you to meet your replacement, Aurana." His dark eyes glinted, "Ivory, your services are no longer required." Her eyes widened in disbelief as he laughed, hearing it echo in her ears, eyes widening.

***

Asuka sighed, resting back in her room. "Man," She whispered, "What a day, so to speak." She closed her eyes, feeling tears form, "I can't believe Lunarias and Kershaw are dead." She wiped them away, "And I didn't even get a chance to get to know them." She sighed, "Why is that girl after me?" She closed her eyes again, letting herself drift off. The door opened, making her sit up, looking around, "Oh! Kursed, it's you."

Kursed smiled at her, mismatched eyes twinkling, "Of course." He came closer to her, "I have to apologize, for earlier."

She looked away, "It's alright. You probably had something you had to do, right."

He gave a nervous laugh, "Yeah, right." He ran a hand through his hair, "But I am sorry, though." He came up to her, helping her stand up, "I should have stopped her."

She smiled, 'There was nothing you could do." Her eyes twinkled, "But it's the thought that counts." She looked up into his eyes, feeling herself go dizzy for a second, swaying slightly.

He chuckled, catching her, "You okay?"

She laughed, "Yeah." She looked back into his eyes, feeling almost sleepy. She tried to smile, "You know, it kinda feels....like I'm sleepy....all of a sudden." She blinked several times, "Kursed...what's...going...on...?" She fell forward, letting out a soft sigh.

Kursed caught her, steadying her. He laughed, bringing her close to him. He moved several strands of hair from her throat. "I'm sorry, Asuka," he whispered, moving closer, baring his fangs, "Please, forgive me."

Chapter 7

Kursed came closer, softly kissing the pulsing vein on her throat. Baring his fangs, he swiftly bent down, sinking them deep into her neck. She let out a startled cry, eyes wide, before closing them again, head dropping back. Kursed closed his eyes letting his mind wander as he drank.

The doorknob turned, slowly opening, "Hey, Asuka, are you-?" Thane broke off, mouth wide, "Kursed?!"

Kursed looked up, letting go of Asuka, watching her fall to the floor with a soft sound.

He smiled nervously, licking his lips, "Heh, heh, Thane, long time, no talk, right?"

Thane rushed to her side, gently picking her up of the floor. He turned her head left and right, checking her neck. There, on the left side, was a small wound, bleeding lightly. He growled, gently placing her onto the bed. He whirled around on Kursed, gripping his collar, "What did you do?!"

Kursed's eyes widened, "Easy, easy, Thane! I swear, I wasn't trying to-!"

Thane snarled, lifting him up off the ground, eyes blazing, "You were in here, drinking her blood! Just what were you trying to do?!"

Kursed stared into his eyes, which were almost pure black. His eyes widened to the size of saucers, as blood red tears began to fall, "I'm…I'm…" He hung his head, "I was trying to take her blood." He looked back up at him, "I'm…I'm….sorry!"

Thane looked away, growling in disgust, "Pull yourself together." He dropped Kursed, sighing, "Man," he held his head in his hand, "You're more trouble than you're worth, Kursed."

Kursed looked up at him, eyes wide, "Thane, I…"

"Go to the Rehabilitation room," Thane said, not looking at him, "Take care of yourself there." He walked over to Asuka, sitting next to her, "Well, what are you waiting for, Kursed? Go."

Kursed quickly nodded, eyes filled with shame. He quietly wiped the blood red tears away, scrambling to his feet, "Thane, thank…thank you! Thank you so much!"

Thane gently moved a few strands of hair from her face, refusing to look at him. He growled, voice inhuman, "Go."

Kursed have a nervous laugh, "Right. Sure. Sorry." He took off, running out the door, and down the hall.

Thane looked toward the door, then back at Asuka, eyes softening. Soft footsteps made him jump, looking up. Lilan stood at the doorway, eyes wide, "Thane? Is she alright?"

"Lilan," He narrowed his eyes, "Get me two small bowls, and fill one with water. I need a cloth, and a bandage." He sighed, "Looks like this is going to be a long night."

***

Kursed quickly made his way to the reinforced door, breathing hard. *'Why?'* He thought, eyes wide, *Why did I attack her like that?* He sighed, bowing his head, *It was her blood. It was pure, free of any impurities'* He let out a small laugh, *She's never lied, done any drugs, anything wrong or sinful.* He opened the door, seeing a small figure inside.

Meagen looked up at him, eyes wide, "Kursed! Oh! Um, I didn't know you'd be coming here! What's wrong?"

Kursed pinched the bridge of his nose, sighing hard, "It's nothing. I…I just need the room for a bit, that's all."

Meagen narrowed her eyes, "Kursed, what happened?"

He walked over to a long table, stretching out onto it, while closing his eyes, "I just went after Asuka's blood."

Meagen went over to him, grabbing a small headset. She gently placed it atop of Kursed head, making sure it was on tight. She ruffled his hair slightly, "Just relax, Kursed. I'll take care of you." She walked over to a small board connected to a small screen.

Kursed opened his eyes, looking over at her, "I just wish…I had never smelt her blood." He looked away, voice filled with shame, "If I hadn't, I wouldn't have attacked her." He gave her a small smile, "Does this make me a horrible person?"

Meagen shook her head, gently touching his cheek, "No, Kursed." She chuckled softly, "It doesn't." She pressed a small button on the board, "Now, relax. We'll get rid of those dark thoughts," She bowed her head, "Otherwise, Xanatos can use them against you."

He have her a small smile, "Thanks." He closed his eyes, letting his head fall to his side.

Meagen walked over to him, stopping near his face. "No, Kursed," She whispered, "Thank you, for stealing my heart." A blood red tear slipped down her cheek as she bent down, gently kissing his cheek.

***

Lilan reentered the room, balancing several items in her small hands. "Here," She handed him the items, while keeping her eyes on Asuka. Asuka moaned, eyes scrunched in pain.

Thane quickly took them, nodding, "Thank you." He started to pick up Asuka, "Now, hold her shoulders, to keep her from falling." Lilan nodded, jumping onto the bed, and holding Asuka up.

He gently touched her chin, lifting it up. "This may sting a little," He whispered, "So, I'm sorry." He gently kissed the small wound, and began to suck out the venom.

Asuka's body tensed up, as she let out a loud cry of pain. "Th…ane," She tried to speak, to get his attention, but she failed, letting out another loud cry of pain.

Thane brought his head away, spitting out the contaminated blood into the empty bowl. "Lilan," He said, "Let her go."

She nodded, "Alright." She quickly got out from under Asuka, letting her body drop.

Thane caught her, slipping an arm around her back and pulling her close. He lifted his head back up, gently shaking her, "Asuka, what is it?"

She tried to keep her eyes open, to speak, "Thane….it burns….all over…."

He gently shushed her as she started to shake, eyes scrunched up in pain, "Asuka, everything will be fine. I promise." He bent his head down over her throat again, pressing his lips against the wound, continuing to suck out the venom. She cried out again, trying to pull away, but Thane held on tight.

Please, He thought, *Just bear with me, Asuka. I know that it hurts, but bear with me. Just once.* He pulled away, spitting out the venom into the bowl. He turned back, for the last time, sucking at the wound. A small, pure droplet touched his tongue, making him jolt up, breathing hard. Gently, he placed her back against the pillows, now dabbing at the wound with a damp cloth.

Lilan looked back at him, eyes wide, "Is she going to be okay?"

He nodded, sighing, "Yeah, she will be." He reached over for the bandage, taping her up.

Lilan didn't look away, "What happened to make you jump like that?"

He shook his head, "Not now, Lilan." He sighed, "Please go and check on Kursed. See if he's doing his time."

She nodded, "Of course." She started for the door, "Oh, please let me know when she wakes up."

He nodded, "You'll be the first." She smiled, leaving the room.

He looked back at Asuka, eyes narrowed. "What is it about you?" He mused, "That made me jump?" He shook his head, "Rest now. I'll watch over you." He walked over to a small chair, sat down, and started to rest.

***

Lilth nodded, listening to Deacon. "Yes," She mused, "To be frank,

I am sorry about your loss. Kershaw was like a brother to me." She sighed, "But to lose another shadow user. Lunarias will be missed." She shook her head.

"If I may ask," Deacon said, "But isn't Thane your strongest shadow user?"

Lilth nodded, "One of the best." She chuckled, "I remember the very day he came here, drenched from the rain. He looked like he had gotten into a fight, for he was scraped up pretty badly." She narrowed her eyes, "He looked up at me with those deadly eyes, and begged for me to let him in, to let him join us." She looked at him, "Almost like you did, Deacon."

He looked away, eyes hard, "We are not alike. Not even close."

Lilth looked away, "Well, be that as it may, you have to get back to Lynx, who I am sure is grieving as you are. And I have my duties to take care of." She waved at him, "You're dismissed."

He bowed, "Thank you, you're majesty." He bowed out of the throne room.

Two soft, gentle hands tenderly wrapped around his arms, chuckling softly, "Hello, Deacon." She gripped his shoulders, slamming him hard against the wall.

His eyes widened, staring deep into the crimson eyes of a pale, young woman, "W-who are you?"

Ivory chuckled, "You're nightmare come true." Her crimson eyes began to glow, "Now, listen to my voice, and only my voice." She began to laugh as her eyes began to burn into his own navy blue eyes. She giggled, "Become my puppet. Help lure the girl to me. Become my puppet. Bring the girl to me. Become my puppet. Make her see images, and bring her to me."

***

Thane looked up from his seat, eyes narrowed. Asuka moaned softly, rolling over onto her back. He sighed, remembering the taste of her blood on his tongue. At first, it was bitter, while the venom was trying to take over her body. Then, as her body stopped shaking, a pure droplet reached him, making him jump.

He studied his hand, looking at his small claws. "Why?" He

whispered, "Why did I jump?" He let out a small growl, getting up from his seat and coming closer, nose twitching all the while. Slowly, he removed the small bandage on her throat, revealing two small marks, scabbing over. He quickly licked his lips, lifting her up off the bed, and bending toward her throat.

"Thane!" A voice exclaimed, making him bolt up in surprise, eyes wide.

Kursed stood there, eyes narrowed in suspicion, "What were you about to do to her?"

Thane gave a nervous chuckle, "Oh, um….nothing, nothing at all."

Kursed smirked, "You were going to 'sample' some of her blood, weren't you?" Thane didn't answer, looking away. Kursed let out a bark of a laugh, "You were! I knew it!"

Thane growled, "Shut it, Kursed! It's not funny!"

Kursed shook his head, "No, it means you're normal, that's all." He shrugged, "So, you get a craving for some warm blood, no big deal."

Thane snarled, eyes hard as cold stone, "Easy for you."

Kursed was about to say something, when Asuka slowly sat up, blinking a few times. She shook her head, "Huh?" Her eyes widened, looking toward the door, "Thane? Kursed? What are you doing at the door? Come on in, sillies!"

Kursed gave her a look, "Asuka, we're right here." He tried to put a hand on her shoulder, but Thane pushed it away, shaking his head.

"Kursed," Thane said, "Just be patient. Maybe….whatever's going on will stop, and she'll be back to normal."

Asuka continued to stare at the doorway, eyes wide and glassy. She giggled, "Guys! Wait up!" She quickly leapt out of bed, hurrying for the door.

Kursed leapt after her, but Thane grabbed his arm, shaking his head, "Don't try and stop her. It's dangerous to shock a person while under a trance." He narrowed his eyes, "We follow. Nothing more."

Kursed growled, pulling away, "Fine. But I swear, if one hair is harmed on her head, I'll kill without a second thought."

Thane nodded, "Fair enough." They quietly snuck out the door after her.

She giggled, hearing it echo in the empty hallways, "Thane! Kursed! Come on, don't leave me behind!"

Thane growled softly. Whoever was doing this was going to pay. He vowed it to the shadows, hoping they would help him.

Chapter 8

Asuka giggled as she continued down the empty, dark hallway, quickly picking up the pace. Kursed growled softly, eyes narrowed, "Where is she going?"

"Patience," Thane said, "Wherever she's going, we will follow." He growled softly, cursing under his breath, "Looks like the training room to me."

Kursed's eyes widened, "Why would she head there?" He growled, "I think I know who's responsible for this!" He narrowed his eyes, "Someone devious. Someone from my past." He clenched both of his hands into fists, "And when I get my claws into her, I'll rip into her like a cat post."

"Yeah," Thane agreed, "After we kill this intruder, we'll beef up security." He quickened his pace, "And when I get my hands on Ivory, I'll rip out her throat, and watch her body twitch while she begs for forgiveness with her dying breath as she dies in my arms."

***

Ivory giggled, crimson eyes glinting as she stood next to Deacon. "Good. Very good," She purred, sliding a slim, pale hand under his chin, "She's almost here. Leave her to me. Take care of anyone who gets in your way."

He nodded curtly, "Got it."

Loud clanking made Ivory turn around, eyes widened in surprise. Klax came out of the shadows, eyes blank and unfeeling, "Deacon, who's this?"

Ivory's eyes narrowed in amusement as she slowly slinked over to him. "Well now," She smirked, "Another strong one." She giggled as she started to circle him, "Hmm, yes. Very strong. Could be useful."

Klax let out a soft growl, "I repeat, who are you?"

Ivory let her fingers dance around his shoulders, slowly moving over to his chest, "Mmm, I love a strong vamp."

"What?" He asked, voice calm, "What are you babbling on about?"

She smirked, "And you know what else I love?"

"I'm sure you'll tell me," Klax said.

Her body slinked slowly around toward his front, softly giggling. She brought her face closer to his neck, keeping a tight hold of his shoulders, "I love your blood."

Before he could even speak, she lunged forward, latching onto his throat, growling as he began to scream, as he tried to pull away. She continued to hold on, sinking her fangs in deeper into his neck, growling in victory. After a few moments, she pulled away, tearing off a small chunk of his skin, while letting go of his body. Ivory smiled, watching his body fall, while she licked her crimson-stained lips, slowly feeling small droplets fall down her chin. His body, missing part of his throat, twitched once, twice, before he died. Motionless, scrap of meat.

Ivory smirked as she pulled out a red handkerchief from the inside of her boot swallowing the small chunk of his skin, before smirking, "I actually did like his blood. Perfectly aged. And the color against the stone is so pretty." She perked her head up, wiping the rest of the blood away from her chin. Soft footsteps reached her ears, coming closer. She smiled, "And she's almost here." She licked her lips again, eyes twinkling, "And I can't wait to taste her blood again!" She giggled, walking over to Deacon, "When she comes, let's give her a….proper greeting, shall we?"

***

Asuka came to a stop before two, wide double doors. She reached out, hesitantly at first, stroking the cool metal handle, before opening the door and quickly looking inside, "Thane, Kursed, I'm here!" She left the door open as she quickly ran inside.

Thane's eyes narrowed, "Now's our chance! Go!" They ran forward, hurrying for the door.

Quickly, it slammed shut, locking swiftly into place. Kursed growled, banging into the door, "Asuka! No!"

Thane placed a firm hand on Kursed's shoulder, "Force will not help us. We need to think of another way in."

"What other way in?!" Kursed spat out, "That is the only way in!"

Thane bowed his head, "Think rationally now. You can't force them open." He shook his head, "No, for this, I may have to use my powers to get us in."

Kursed sent him a look, "Work fast, Shadow boy. There's something evil in that room, and it wants revenge."

***

The door slammed shut behind Asuka, quickly locking into place. She jumped, eyes wide. Asuka blinked quickly, shaking her head, "W-where….where am I?"

Ivory let out a soft giggle, taking a step forward, as the shadows clung to her body, "Welcome, small one." She took a few steps back into the shadows, giggling, "I'm going to enjoy breaking you, and gorging myself on your blood." She rushed forward, claws raking deep into Asuka's arm, making her shriek in pain.

Asuka blinked back tears of pain, eyes narrowed, "W-what do you w-want?"

Ivory narrowed her eyes, licking a stray drop of blood off one of her claws. She brought her hand back, raking her nails deep into Asuka's face, "You stole Xanatos away from me!" She brought her leg up, slamming it hard and fast into Asuka's midsection, "You stole the one token of my affection away!" She latched onto the poor girls' hair, throwing her across the room, "You stole away my hope!" Asuka tried to get up, but was kicked across the room by Ivory's boot. Ivory snarled,

"Get up!" She kicked the young girl again, "Get up! Fight back!' Asuka didn't move, "Fight back!"

Asuka took in a shuddering breath as she slowly pulled herself into a sitting position, breathing hard, "Why fight?" She bowed her head, "There's no point to it. All it does is cause more bloodshed, more grief." She looked up, meeting Ivory's eyes, "And you'd kill me if I try." Her eyes blazed with courage, trying to stand up for herself, "So, why bother?"

Ivory growled, eyes wide. *Those eyes,* She thought to herself, *Why stare at me with such eyes filled with determination? With courage?* She looked down at Asuka's hands, which were trembling as they continuously clenched and unclenched into fists, *Of course, she's trying to hide it, to put on a brave front. But inside, she's trembling like a frightened little rabbit. Heh, this should be easy.* She brought her clawed hand back as she growled, swinging it forward.

A slim, pale hand gripped Ivory's wrist, holding it tightly in place. Asuka's eyes widened, taking in the redheaded beauty, "Lynx!"

Lynx smirked, "Sorry I'm late, little kitten." Her crimson eyes hardened like cold rubies, "Now, what are you doing her, little rat?"

Ivory snarled, eyes wild, "None of your business, hag!"

Lynx growled, fangs bared, "We will see." Ivory tried to pull away, but Lynx pulled her back, spinning her around, and bringing her right arm back, "Gonna tell me now?"

Ivory snarled, struggling, "Never!"

Lynx shrugged, "Tried to give you an easy out." She held Ivory's arm a little tighter as she pulled up, grunting slightly. Asuka turned her head away as she heard a loud, sickening crack.

Lynx let Ivory drop to the cold, stony floor, listening quietly as Ivory howled loudly in pain. Ivory snarled, rounding on Lynx while her right arm hung uselessly at her side, "You….you…." She growled softly, trying to think of a good comeback.

Lynx smiled, "Stupid little rat."

Asuka groaned, trying to get up, but slumped back to the ground, breathing hard. "Lynx," She gasped out, trying to stay conscious.

Lynx whirled around, eyes wide, "Asuka!" She dashed over to Asuka's side, helping her up, "Little kitten, are you alright?"

Asuka let out a breath, shaking her head, "No....I....I think she m-might have b-b-broken a few ribs. Ugh, m-my head. Feels like its s-s-swimming in a murky pond."

Lynx placed a gentle arm around her waist, slowly helping her up, "C'mon, let's get you help." She turned around, barely having enough time to see the bright, silver glint of a sword before it came down, slicing deep into Lynx's shoulder. Lynx cried out in pain, blood splattering everywhere. Asuka shielded her face as it splattered all around them. Some landed on her face and hair, while the rest splattered all over her dress.

Ivory smirked, holding her limp arm in a bent position across her chest, grimacing in pain as it slowly began to heal. "You're getting what you deserve, harpy," She spat, voice hoarse, "I hope you burn." She nodded to Deacon.

Asuka's eyes widened, trying to get out of Lynx's grip, "No, please! Deacon!"

A soft, pale hand gently touched her shoulder, causing her to jump softly. Asuka met Lynx's eyes as Lynx smiled, "Do not be afraid, kitten." She bowed her head, "If I must die, then I must." Lynx softly kissed Asuka's cheek, licking the blood that stained her own lips as she pulled away, crimson eyes filled with sorrow, "Be strong, little kitten. I am glad to have met you, and am sorry I couldn't get to know you more."

Ivory's eyes widened, "What do you-? No!" Realizing a split second too late. She watched as Lynx sprinted up, throwing herself against the silver blade. Lynx grunted as her head flew back, back arched, as she fell against the hilt, the light leaving her eyes.

Ivory growled, watching her body slowly fall as Deacon pulled his sword out from her body, hearing a small, squishing sound as he did so, "Serves her right, little wretch. Now," She rounded onto Asuka, "I can finally get rid of you."

Asuka cried out, crawling over to Lynx's side, trying to wake her,

"Lynx!" She shook her shoulder gently, hoping the young beauty would jump up, ready to fight again, "Get up! Get up! Please!"

Lynx didn't move, as blood began to pool forth, blending in with her hair. Ivory chuckled, moving a few strands of raven black hair out of her face, "Now, brat, let's finish this!" She moved forward, claws toward her face.

A slim, silver blade came down, stopping inches from Ivory's throat. Ivory gulped, feeling the blade press slightly into her collarbone. Deacon growled, bright, ice blue eyes blazing with cold fire, "Back off of her." Ivory didn't move, narrowing her eyes, "Are you deaf? Now!"

Ivory carefully slinked out from his blade, swallowing her growl, "You snapped outta it, huh?" Ivory chuckled, "Pity. You would have made a beautiful puppet." She looked down at Asuka, who was too shocked to even speak, let alone utter a single word. While Lynx's body lay motionless, a large, gaping hole, where blood continued to pool out.

Ivory sighed, "As much as I'd love to stay and kill you two, I'm afraid I've done enough damage for one night." She sent Asuka a look, eyes cold and hard, "Enjoy every breath you take, young one, 'cause I'll be back. And when I return, you're mine." She took a few steps back into the shadows, chuckling softly.

Asuka refused to move, until Deacon called out to her, voice ringing loud and clear, "Asuka."

Asuka's head slowly turned to look at him, eyes empty and hollow, "Yes, Deacon."

Deacon kept his head bowed, "Stop your crying. Lynx will never come back."

Asuka growled, eyes wide, "You can at least hope she might! What good is it to lose hope over losing your loved ones? You can only hope that they are with you in spirit."

Deacon lowered his head, breathing hard, "True." He chuckled, "But, I know she won't come back. She's have *passed on*."

"Passed on?" Asuka growled, "No, that can't be! Deacon!" Her eyes widened, "Deacon, please!"

He sighed, looking away, "Somehow, hearing that, though, I know it will happen. You….have wonderful friends who love and care about you. Keep them close." He looked over at Lynx, chuckling softly. "It's not fair, Lynx," His voice became soft, "Why did you have to die?" Slowly, he reached over for the blade, already stained with Lynx's blood.

Asuka's eyes widened, rushing over and gripping his arm, "No, Deacon! Please!" She gripped the blade in her hands, drawing blood, which made her wince in pain.

Deacon growled, pushing her roughly away. Asuka cried out, landing hard onto the cold ground. Quickly, he held the hilt up into the air, blade pointed down. With two, blood red tears falling down his cheeks, he threw the blade forward with a sickening, "crack." With a final sigh, his body slowly began to fall to the ground, breathing stilled.

The double doors finally flew open, revealing an exhausted Kursed and Thane. Their eyes widened, taking in the sight of the two bodies. Asuka looked up at them, body shaking as hot, salty tears began to fall, mingling with the blood on her cheeks. "Thane," She whispered, "Kursed, I'm sorry. I…couldn't save them."

Chapter 9

Asuka remained frozen as Thane and Kursed stood there, eyes wide. "Kursed," Thane said, voice low.

Kursed blinked in surprise. Shaking his head, he looked over at Thane, "Yes?"

Thane walked over to Asuka, gently scooping her up into his arms, "I'm going to take her to the Hospital Wing," He bowed his head, eyes narrowed, "You know what to do with the bodies."

Kursed bowed his head, sighing, "Yeah." He didn't bother looking over at them, "Just....get Asuka out of here." He growled, "Whoever did this is going to pay."

Thane nodded slowly, "Alright, Kursed." He turned to leave.

Asuka finally found her voice again, stopping both Thane and Kursed, "Please, wait."

Kursed looked over at Asuka, eyes narrowed, "Yes?"

Asuka lowered her gaze, "I really am sorry for your loss."

Kursed's gaze softened as he reached out toward the frightened mortal and gently ruffled up her hair, "Hey, they were sacrificed in the line of duty." He smiled gently, "There was nothing you could have done."

Thane cleared his throat, voice hard "As touching as it would be to have a nice, cozy little sharing circle, I believe I need to get Asuka to the Hospital Wing, otherwise," He looked back down at Asuka, "Her wounds are going to get worse."

Kursed nodded quickly, "Right, right." He waved a pale hand, "Go on. I can handle things here." Thane sent him a hard look, before leaving.

Sighing deeply, with a heavy heart, Kursed looked back at the two bodies, eyes wide and glassy. Eyes flashing slightly, flames shot up around them, crackling merrily. He felt his heart wrench as the fire claimed both Lynx and Deacon, the lovers, and the emotionless Klax, the flames' light catching briefly in their blank stares. Kursed chuckled softly to himself, thinking. Why was he felling these feelings? Feelings of regret, of sorrow. He was a vampire, for Christs' sake, a blood sucking demon of the night.

He had a feeling he knew what was going in with him, and he wouldn't be satisfied until he was sure he was right. Closing his eyes against the flames, he let two, small blood red rivers fall down his face, as a final moment to those who were lost.

***

Asuka squirmed in Thane's grasp, eyes narrowed in annoyance, "Thane, I can walk." No answer, "Thane." Once again, no answer, "Thane!"

He looked down at her, stone grey eyes hard, "What?"

She gritted her teeth, "I….can walk."

He made a small little noise of disbelief as he smirked, "Suit yourself." He gently set her down onto her feet, "Forgive me for trying to help."

She shot him a look, "If I wanted your help, I would have asked." She went to take a step forward, but winced, eyes scrunched up in pain.

Thane stepped over to her, chuckling softly, "Need some help?"

She quickly shook her head, biting her lip, "N-no. I'm…quite capable of walking…on my own." She took another step, once again, wincing in pain.

Thane laughed gently, "Need some help, princess?"

Asuka gave him a hard look, eyes shooting daggers at him, "No, I don't."

He ran a hand through his hair, sighing, "Jeez, you're more trouble than you're worth." He quickly strode over to her, and scooped her up, carrying her the rest of the way, while ignoring the swears and complaints she threw at him.

Asuka continued to struggle, "Put me down, Thane!" She growled, "Put me down!" She cast daggers at him, growling in anger and annoyance.

Thane reached over and opened the door in front of him, grunting as he did so, "Meagen!" He strode through the door, growling softly, "You there?"

Meagen poked her head through a small office door, hazel eyes wide with surprise, "Yes, Thane?" She let out a small cry as Thane laid Asuka down onto a nearby cot. She sent him an icy look, "Just what did you do to her?"

Thane let out a small snort, "I didn't do anything!"

She snarled, "Then who did?"

Thane shook his head, "Some intruder tramp."

Asuka sighed, "I honestly don't need all this. I'm perfectly fine." She went to move, but winced again in pain, softly crying out.

Meagen made a small clicking noise with her tongue against her teeth, "Figures." She shook her head, "We live in the middle of nowhere, overlooking a city, surrounded by a forest, and yet we have no security around here!"

He sent her a hard look, "I already know we need security around here. Talk to Lilth is you've got a problem."

Meagen shot him a nasty look, before turning back to Asuka, "Now, where does it hurt?"

"Wait," Asuka held up a hand, "You're a healer, too?"

Meagen chuckled softly, "I'm the smart one around here, apparently. Lilth appointed me to the Hospital Wing. Said something about being good at helping people."

Asuka nodded, "Well, better you then him," She jerked her head over at Thane.

Thane made a small, sputtering sound, eyes wide, "And what's wrong with me?!"

Asuka sent him an annoyed look, "You're asking me why?" He looked away, growling softly under his breath.

Meagen looked back at Asuka, smiling softly, "Now, where does it hurt?"

Asuka winced as she lifted her arm up, pointing, "My ribs, mostly. But it's also my arm and my head."

Meagen nodded slowly, "I see." She turned her gaze to Thane, "Would you mind terribly if you left us for a few minutes?"

Thane gave her a quizzical look "Huh?"

Meagen narrowed her eyes, "Go out, and wait in the hall."

"Oh," Thane muttered, "Right." He turned to leave.

Once the door opened, then shut, Meagen turned back to Asuka, "Alright, out of the dress."

Asuka gave her a strange look, "Huh?!"

Meagen giggled softly, "I meant to take it off so I can fix you up." She shook her head, blushing slightly, "What did you think I meant?"

Asuka shook her head, "Never mind." Quickly, she stripped down, getting the ripped, bloody dress off of her chilled skin, "There, go ahead."

Carefully, with gentle fingers, Meagen gently examined Asuka, pushing lightly on several sore spots around her ribs and arms. Asuka let out a small cry several times when Meagen pushed down a little too hard, but the resumed gritting her teeth and sitting in silence.

Meagen clicked her tongue again as her narrowed eyes took in the sight of Asuka's body. Here and there were several cuts still oozing a little bit of blood. In other areas, were dark, colorful bruises. Meagen shook her head again, "Man, whoever got you, got you good."

Asuka sighed, "I know, I know." She chuckled softly, "So, how bad is it?"

"Well," Meagen said, "You're alive, right?" Asuka nodded, "You do have some broken ribs, and several scrapes and cuts, but all in all, you're alive." She giggled, "Lemme get you some bandages, and bandage you up." She walked over to the small cabinet next to the cot, grabbing several cloth bandages.

Asuka curled herself up into a small ball, wincing in pain as she did so, "Meagen, can I ask you a question?"

"You just did," Meagen smirked, eyes twinkling as she came back to Asuka, "Just kidding, fire away."

"What brought you to Lilth and the others?" Asuka asked, "Any why are you the cook, and the residential nurse?" She blushed softly, "Sorry. That was two questions."

Meagen giggled softly, "No, it's quite alright." She cleared her throat, "Arms up, if you please." Asuka acknowledged her, "Meagen unwrapped a portion of the small cloth, and began to wrap it around her, "To answer your first question, I ran away from the enemy. I….I was a slave for Xanatos. Kind of like his little plaything." She smirked, "Enough was enough, so I ran for it."

Asuka winced as Meagen pulled tightly on the cloth, "Ouch!"

Meagen's eyes widened, "Oh, did I get you?"

Asuka shook her head, "N-no, I'm fine."

Meagen chuckled softly, "To answer your second question, Lilth saw my qualities, and appointed me to these spots."

"Ouch!" Asuka said, grunting as Meagen took a few clips and pinned the bandage together.

Meagen smiled, "There, all done." The door opened again, causing both Asuka and Meagen to look up, eyes wide.

***

Thane sighed as he slipped outside for a moment, feeling stressed and drained. A small feeling in the back of his head started to pound, bugging him. He knew he would need substance soon. Slowly, he ran his tongue over his elongated incisors. He took a small intake of breath, before releasing it.

Soft footsteps make Thane jump slightly, cursing under his breath. Lilth chuckled, "Surprised to see me, Thane?"

He gave her a small smile, "Not really. Had my guard down for a moment, that's all."

She smiled, eyes twinkling, "That's rare to see, Thane actually had his guard down for once."

He sent her a look, "You're amused by the smallest things, aren't you?"

"Isn't it obvious?" Lilth giggled softly. She grew serious, "You have to feed soon, don't you?"

"Isn't it obvious?" Thane joked, smiling slightly.

She clapped her hands together in glee, "And he's actually smiling and making jokes! What brought this all about?"

"I believe you asked me a question," He shook his head, "Yeah, I have to feed, and soon. Otherwise…" He trailed off, voice dying.

She nodded, "Of course. We don't need that." She sighed, "Take Kursed with you. He'll need to feed as well." Her eyes narrowed, "Plenty of criminals hide in these woods. Plenty of sustenance."

"Was there something you needed?" Thane asked, growing more and more annoyed.

She shook her head, blinking in surprise, "Oh! Forgive me." She cleared her throat, "I've talked it over with the others, and they've volunteered to help train Asuka once she's patched up."

His eyes narrowed in surprise, "But she's wounded."

"Exactly," Lilth said, "The enemy is not going to sit around, twiddling their thumbs and wait, will they?"

He shook his head, "But…I…I don't want to…" He trailed off again, eyes downcast.

"To what?" Lilth asked, "Hurt her?" She chuckled again, "So, you truly do have a conscious, don't you?"

He sighed, looking away, "I've always had one, I had just buried it deep down inside me for so long."

She moved a few bangs out of his face, smiling softly, "Thane, do you resent becoming what you are?"

He sighed softly, "I resent my sire, but not what I have become." He shook his head, "I still remember what she told me….the night I made my first kill."

"You are a predator, just like a wolf or a shark. You've had a taste of it, and you'll taste it again. You can run, but you can never hide from your hunger."

Lilth placed a cool hand on his hot cheek, "Forget about her, she brought you up in darkness. You came to us, and to the light." She walked over to the double doors, "Well, Thane, shall we tell Asuka our plan?"

He nodded, swallowing hard, "Yeah, of course." Lilth smiled as she firmly grasped the doors, and pulled them open.

Meagen and Asuka looked up, eyes wide. "Oh," Meagen said, "Lilth, hello."

Lilth bowed her head in politeness, "Hello, Meagen." She looked over at Asuka, smiling softly, "How do you feel, child?"

Asuka gave a weak smile, "I feel like I wrestled a lycan, and lost."

Lilth bowed her head, "I do apologize about that. I tried to keep everything that happened to you quiet, but, the whole mansion found out."

"How," Asuka asked, curious.

"Everyone heard Thane and Kursed trying to break down the training room doors," Lilth said, "Guess curiosity gets the better of them, huh?"

Asuka nodded, "I'd rather have told them face to face, though."

Lilth smiled, "Well, you'll get your chance. They've all volunteered to train you."

Asuka's eyes widened, "But…shouldn't I have time to at least heal?"

Lilth shook her head, "The enemy will not just sit around and wait for any one of us to be healed. It's better to start training now, to prepare you in case you get attacked again."

Asuka nodded, knowing there was no arguing with the old vampire, "Yes, Lilth."

Lilth turned to leave, but stopped, "Oh, there is one more thing."

Asuka nodded again, "What is it?"

Lilth's crimson eyes narrowed as she locked eyes with Asuka's own bright ones, "Since it was both Kursed and Thane who saved you, it has to be one of them who will sire you."

There was a soft noise at the double doors, which drew everyone's' attention away from Asuka. Lilan stood there, eyes wide with a small hand pressed against her mouth, "You….you want to sire Asuka?"

Lilth slowly nodded, "If she is sired, then she may stand a chance against another attack."

Thane smiled, ruffling the small girls' hair, "Don't worry, kiddo. She'll be fine."

She frowned, looking up at him, "You promise?" She held up a hand before he could speak "Pinky swear and cross your heart!"

He chuckled softly, amused by Lilan's childish antics. The child may look twelve, but she had the personality of a seven-year old. Which was cute, don't get him wrong, but it almost always got on his nerves, "Sure." He crossed pinkies with her, twisting them, then finally raised a hand up and made a small mark over his chest.

She pulled her hand away, satisfied, "There, you promised. And you can't break your promise."

He laughed softly, "Alright, alright. Take it easy, Lil."

Lilth narrowed her eyes, remembering something else, "Oh, another thing."

Asuka looked over at Lilth, gently biting her lip as she spoke, voice slightly shaky, "What....what is it?"

Lilth gently smiled as she spoke, voice low, "Before you can be sired, you must watch Thane or Kursed make a fresh kill, and take part in feeding, to prove you want to be sired."

Chapter 10

Thane looked over at Asuka, eyes narrowed in annoyance, "Come on, we don't have all night."

Asuka shot him a hard look, wincing slightly, "I'm working on it."

He shook his head, rolling his eyes, "Humans." He walked over to her and scooped her up, carrying her over his shoulder, "Much better."

She squirmed, calling him every name in the book she could think of, "Put me down!" Thane ignored her, which made her growl even more, "Let me go!"

Thane reached out, pulling open the heavy, metallic door, and stepping inside, "Knock off your squirming, will ya?" He gently set her down, "There, you're safe."

Kursed came up quietly toward then, smiling softly, "Nice to see you two. Now, we can begin." He clapped his hands, lights flaring on.

The room was huge, filled with all sorts of equipment. In one corner was a small ring, big enough for two people to spar. In another corner were several weights of all different sizes, some on bars, others littering the ground. Balance beams and rings were in different areas, with Meagen slowly doing her rounds on one. She waved to them, "Hello."

There were also several hanging punching bags and kickboxing dummies, with boxing gloves strewn all over. Asuka shook her head, eyes wide, "Whoa."

Kursed nodded, smiling, "It's not much, but it works."

Asuka shook her head, trying to clear her muddled thoughts, "I...I..." She trailed off, trying to think of what to say.

Thane put a hand on her shoulder, "Now, where to begin?"

The door opened, and then closed, soft footsteps making their way over to them. Lilan looked up at Thane, eyes narrowed, "You guys left without me."

Asuka gently knelt down beside the small girl, smiling softly, "I'm sorry, Lilan." She cast a look over at Thane, "Somebody had to hurry me over here."

Thane looked away, "Don't blame me, brat. Lilth wanted to get your training started."

Kursed started to chuckle, eyes twinkling, "Wow, Thane."

Thane rounded on Kursed, making a small, sputtering sound, "What's that supposed to mean?"

Kursed shrugged, "Well, I just didn't know that you acted more like a stubborn child. I guess Lilan is rubbing off on you."

"Enough," Asuka held up both of her hands, trying to get them to stop, "Kursed, don't tease Thane. Thane, don't listen to Kursed."

Kursed placed a hand on Asuka's shoulder, laughing softly, "Well, we kinda can't do that."

She gave him a puzzled look, "Why not?"

Kursed strolled over to Thane, clasping a hand on his shoulder, "Thane's my master in a way. Whatever he tells me to do, I have to do it."

Asuka's eyes widened as many thoughts ran through her head, thoughts that included Thane and Kursed in ways she would have never imagined.

Kursed's eyes widened, "Not like that, silly." He sighed, "I just listen to his commands is all."

Lilan cleared her throat, "Hey!"

Asuka looked down at Lilan, "Yes?"

Lilan tapped her foot, impatience showing in her eyes, "Aren't we supposed to be training Asuka?"

Thane nodded, "Right, right. This way." He walked over to the balance beam that Meagen was practicing on, motioning for her to step off. He gestured to Asuka, "Alright, show us what you can do."

Her eyes were wide, "Huh?"

He sighed, pinching the bridge of his nose, "Get up there and show us that you can balance."

Her face turned red as she gently shook her head, "Oh, I knew that."

Thane gestured to the beam, "Well, what are you waiting for?"

She blinked in surprise, "Sorry." She sauntered over to the beam and leapt onto it, wincing slightly. Grunting, she stood up, and began to flex, twisting and turning this way and that.

Meagen's eyes were wide, "You're good."

Asuka sent her a small smile, "Thanks. My mother made me take gymnastics when I was younger."

Thane made a small noise as he looked away, eyes narrowed, "Spoiled."

Asuka shot him a look, "What's that supposed to mean?"

He rolled his eyes, "Nothing, nothing at all."

Meagen let out a small, nervous giggle, stepping in between the fighting duo, "N-now, now, let's not fight, you two."

Both of them rounded on Meagen, eyes wide, "Who asked you?!"

Meagen turned a deep shade of red, looking away, "No one."

There was a loud, piercing cry as a black blur rushed past them, running over to Asuka and bowled her over, causing her to let out a small cry. She gritted her teeth as she struggled to get back up onto her feet. Turning her gaze over, she saw a familiar looking twin cuddled up to her, gripping her arm, eyes twinkling, "Mmm, Asuka."

Her body tensed, eyes wide, "C-C-Cyrus?!"

He smiled, looking up at her, "Of course."

Asuka grunted as her other side was weighted down. Slowly, her gaze slid over to see Kursed nuzzled up to her other arm, smiling, "Kursed?!"

He sent her a sly smirk, "Who else?"

Her breathing quickened as both boys trapped her, nuzzling in close. Asuka looked over at Thane, reaching out to him, "H-help, m-m-me."

Thane rolled his eyes, growling. Reaching out with both hands, he gripped the scruff of their shirts and yanked them up into the air, making them both yelp out in surprise. Kursed sent Thane a wide-eyed look, "Lemme go!"

Thane shrugged, "As you wish." He dropped both boys to the ground, landing hard on their backsides.

Cyrus growled, "You didn't have to do it *that* way!"

Thane shook his head, "Whatever."

Lilan growled, "Can we continue?"

Meagen nodded quickly, "Of course, of course." She looked over at Asuka, "I guess balance is out of the question."

Thane curled his lip, "Because *mommy* paid to have princess learn gymnastics."

Asuka growled, rounding on him, "Shut up about her! You don't even know her!"

Meagen quickly clashed Asuka's shoulders, "Easy now. Why don't we move onto stealth?"

Asuka nodded, "Y-yeah, sure."

Cyrus grinned, "Excellent!" He took her wrist within his hand and pulled her over to a small side of the room. He pointed over to the corner, "Stand there."

She obeyed, puzzled, "How do we do this?"

Cyrus smiled, "Well, all I have to do is stay silent and grade you on how well you can get past my bro." He gestured over to a large wolf with grayish-silver fur, and glowing yellow eyes. Ringing around his legs were black, lightning-like symbols, leading down to black paws. A small tuft of fur hung in his eyes, giving him a roguish look.

Asuka gulped, eyes Cyro, "I...I have to get past...him?"

Cyrus chuckled, "Remember, to pass, you can't make any noise. Otherwise, you'll have to start all over again."

She gave him a curt nod, "Alright. I...I can do this!" She watched the large wolf as he curled up onto the ground, and closed his eyes. She took in a deep breath, before stepping forward, easily placing a foot down. He didn't move. She took another step, then another. Placing a foot down, she kicked a small stone aside, alerting the large wolf, making him snarl.

She jumped back, crying out, "What did I do?"

Cyrus smirked, "My guess is that you took a wring step. Try again."

Asuka sighed, "Fine." She walked back over to the corner, waiting for Cyro to fall back into his position, closing his eyes. She sighed before taking a step, then another. She took a step, bringing her foot down. Cyro shot up and started snarling.

Cyrus chuckled softly, "We can try again soon. Why don't you move onto combat?"

She nodded, biting her lip, "Sure…I guess."

Lilan came up to her, gripping Asuka's hand in her own small one, "C'mon! This way!" Lilan pulled her over to the small ring, sparring mats here and there around it.

Kursed smiled, "Thank you for joining us, Asuka." He came closer to her, "Now, what Lilan and I are going to do is come at you easy, so you can warm up, and then fight for real."

Asuka nodded, "A-alright." She took a defensive stance, "I'm ready."

Lilan ran forward, bringing her fist back and pushing it forward, aiming for Asuka's ribs. Asuka danced left, keeping her eyes on Lilan's small, yet agile form. Lilan matched her step for step, bringing her knee up, eyes narrowed. Asuka brought up her own leg, blocking Lilan's own. Lilan bounced back, leaping into the air, and swinging a clawed hand down, ready to claw Asuka's face. Asuka ducked, pivoting on her right foot, and kicking Lilan in the small of her back.

Kursed leapt forward and started with a volley of punches, quicker for any normal line of vision to see. Asuka cried out, moving this way and that to avoid getting hit. He brought up an elbow, bringing it down toward her face. Asuka reached out and blocked the hit, bouncing back from the force of the blow. He grunted, bringing his foot up, skimming the skin on her nose. She cried out, eyes wide, "I like my face the way it is, thanks! Don't rearrange it!"

Kursed smirked, raising up his fist and aimed for her ribs. Asuka spun away and brought up her foot, kicking him down. He fell, grunting in surprise. He turned around, looking up at her and smiling, "Guess you do know how to fight."

Asuka's face colored slightly, looking away, "They did teach me a bit at the academy."

A foot lashed out, kicking her roughly in her backside. She cried out, sprawling onto of Kursed. Kursed chuckled softly, meeting her eyes, "Wow, I never pegged you for the dominant, forceful type, Asuka. If you wanted me that badly, all you had to do was ask."

She socked him in the arm, "It wasn't on purpose, I assure you." She got up and faced Thane, "He was the one who kicked me."

Thane shrugged, "So what if I did?" His eyes met hers, challenging her, "Gonna do something about it?"

She growled, feeling the same, boiling anger rise within her, adding to her annoyance. Without a single word, she threw herself at him, bringing a slim hand back, and ramming it hard into his jaw, surprising him. She narrowed her eyes in satisfaction, "There, problem solved." She started to turn back to Kursed and Lilan, when Thane reached out, gripping her arm in a vice-like grip, pulling her back.

He growled, "Oh no, you don't." He brought his fist back, quickly throwing it forward. Asuka dodged, breathing hard. Again and again, his fists came at her, aiming for her blind sides.

She grunted, eyes wide as she dodged his foot. *He's fast,* She thought, *Extremely fast.* She dodged another fist, this time, close to her cheek, *If he keeps this up,* She panted, trying to focus, *I'll end up severely hurt, or worse.*

He sidestepped to her side, elbowing her back, which made her cry out in surprise. Quickly, he slammed his knee up, knocking the wind out of her. She looked up at him, trying to make a sound, but none came out. She grunted as a fist collided with her ribs. Her body shook, as pain jolted throughout her body. Thane knelt to the ground, sweeping the space at her feet, knocking her off balance.

She shakily tried to stand up, but fell to the ground, breathing hard. She looked up to see Thane's fist speeding toward her midsection. Eyes that were once a steely grey were now as black as the night. She let out a small cry as it connected with her ribs, the sound of breaking bones in the air. She fell back to the ground, meters away from everyone, wheezing for air.

"Asuka?"

"Asuka!"

"Asuka, can you hear me?"

The voices all rang at once, echoing in her head. She looked up at Thane, who just stood there, eyes wide, now their familiar shade of grey. Something hot and wet started to run down the front of her body. Reaching down toward her midsection, she gently placed a hand on the spot, pulling it away. Blood, scarlet against her skin, was all she saw.

Thane looked down at his own hands, which were stained with the same crimson against her clothes. His gaze shifted over to her, trying to speak, "Asuka…I…I'm sorry."

She tried to speak, but no sound came out. Blinding, white-hot pained stabbed at her as she tried to breathe. Kursed came forward and scooped her up carefully into his arms, letting out a breath, "Asuka needs to rest. She can train some more tomorrow." Refusing to look at Thane, he strode toward the door.

Lilan ran forward, gripping one of the handles and pulling it open, letting Kursed, Meagen, and the twins to step out first. Lilan cast Thane a last, final look, before excusing herself as well.

Thane took a few, shaky breaths, while looking back down at his blood-stained hands. *What….what happened to me'* He thought to himself, *I…I just…lost it and attacked her!* He shook his head, trying to clear his thoughts, but they stayed, *I…I didn't mean to lost it! I…I promised myself I wouldn't harm her!* He sniffed the air, a strong urge of desire came over him, *What….what is that wonderful smell?* He sniffed again, drinking the unknown scent in deep, *It…it smells like something untainted, full of life and purity.* He looked down at his hands, taking in the sight of red. Closing his eyes, he brought one of his hands, sniffing it. Slowly, his tongue ran over the liquid, relishing the taste.

It tasted familiar to him, along with the scent. Who did it belong to, though? He closed his eyes, feeling his thoughts rush back to him in a heartbeat, remembering how the blood got there, and whose it was.

Asuka.

***

There was a small knock on Asuka's door, startling Asuka out of the book from the small shelf near her bed. Marking her place, she closed it and put it aside, "Come in."

Both Thane and Kursed stepped inside her room, Thane shutting her door. Kursed smiled at her, "Hey, how are you doing?"

Asuka smiled weakly at him, "A little better." Her face colored slightly, "I'm sorry....for earlier."

Kursed chuckled, "What for?" He shot a look toward Thane, "Shadow boy over there should have been in control."

Thane snarled, "Watch it, fire puppet. I'm still stronger than you."

Kursed held up his hands, "Take it easy, Thane, it was just a joke."

Asuka cleared her throat, trying to get their attention, "Did you guys need something?"

Kursed sat down next to her, chuckling softly, "Lilth told us one of us had to sire you." He brought her close, nuzzling her cheek, "I sure hope you choose me, Asuka."

She socked him hard in his arm, making him let go in surprise, crying out, "I don't have to choose anyone!"

Kursed narrowed his eyes, "Lilth said otherwise." His eyes widened in surprise, "Oh, almost forgot!" He turned to look at Thane, "You got something to say, Thane?"

Thane nodded curtly, coming closer to her bed. He sat down, head bowed, "Forgive me....for earlier." He shook his head, "I didn't mean to lose control."

She smiled, taking his hand in her slim, cool ones, "It's okay. I kinda figured you lost control. I mean, your eyes change."

He sighed, running a hand through his hair, "That happens....when I lose control."

Kursed cleared his throat, making them both jump in surprise, "We have to figure out who's going to sire Asuka, remember?"

Thane nodded quickly, "Right, right."

Asuka turned her gaze toward Thane, trying to keep her voice steady, "H-how do you...sire others?"

Thane chuckled, moving closer to her, as his eyes locked onto her own. "Well, I would take you gently into my arms," He wrapped his arms slowly around her, mindful of her injuries. "Then, I would sink my fangs deep into your pretty throat," He brought his face down to her throat, softly kissing a vein.

She sucked in a breath. He was doing this on purpose, why, she didn't know. She could feel his hot breath against her neck as he chuckled softly, "No, I'm not doing this on purpose. You asked." He nuzzled the crook of her neck, taking in her scent, as his mind began to cloud over, "I would take my fill from you, until you fell into the brink of life and death, the venom beginning to take over your body. If I chose to, I would give you some of my own lifeblood. If you can, you drink. The blood, mingled with the venom, starts the change, which is painful." He pulled his head away, eyes narrowed, "That's it."

Asuka's eyes remained cloudy, hardly breathing. She quickly shook her head, blinking rapidly. She let out a small breath, "W-wow" Her voice remained shaky, 'You certainly know how to cast a spell."

He chuckled softly, "One of my many qualities."

Kursed cleared his throat, "Hey, I have an idea."

They both looked over at him. "What?" Asuka asked.

His eyes met Thane's smirking, "Why don't we share out experiences with Asuka? Ease her into the change?"

Thane nodded slowly, "If she wants to hear them."

Asuka nodded quickly, "Of course! I'd love to!"

Kursed smiled, eyes twinkling, "Alright. I'll go first."

Chapter 11

Kursed strode through the college courtyard, hearing the bells echo around him, "I'm so late!" He shook his head, "Why did I stay up last night? Stupid studying!" He growled, putting on more speed. He bowed his head, looking down at his timetable, "Why do I have Physics right now?"

He rounded the fountain, feeling its light spray gently wash over his face. He looked up just in time to see a young girl round the other side of the fountain, eyes wide, "Hey, watch out!" She flung up her arms, covering her face as he tried to stop, tried to keep from hitting the young girl, but to no avail. Both of them smacked hard into each other, crying out in surprise.

Kursed landed hard on his side, feeling his body jolt with pain. He groaned, shaking his head, "What hit me?" His eyes widened, remembering the young girl who had smacked into him. He sat up quickly, reaching over to her, taking in her appearance. She had long, silky black hair and chestnut brown eyes. Her lips were full and parted, slightly pink. She wore nothing on her body but black, the top reaching down to her navel, stretched tight over her skin.

She smiled, teeth white and straight, "Sorry, I wasn't paying attention. I was in a hurry."

Kursed chuckled softly, helping the young beauty stand, "The fault is entirely mine, Miss…?"

The vivacious vixen blushed softly, "Oh, my name is Ivy. And you are?"

Kursed took his hand gently in his and softly kissed it. "I'm…" He racked his brains, unsure if he should give out his first name, for fear of her shying away, "Allen, *enceinte, mademoiselle.*"

She giggled softly, "Well, Mister Allen, seems I've found myself a gentleman."

He shook his head, "I'm no gentleman, Miss Ivy."

She brought up two fingers and started to trail them up his arm, sending small, delicious shivers up his spine. He tried to speak, but no sound came out. He shook his head, clearing his thoughts. Ivy giggled, "Cat got your tongue, Allen?"

He ran a hand through his black hair, "Well…I…" He trailed off, face feeling red.

She looked away, "Sorry, Allen, I…I didn't mean to throw myself at you." She cleared her throat, "I suppose I should get going." She turned to leave.

Kursed gently grasped her arm, pulling her back to him, "One minute, please."

Ivy looked his way, eyes wide, "Yes?"

Kursed felt his face grow hot again as he avoided her gaze, "Well…I was wondering…would you…dinner?" He trailed off, eyes wide and hopeful.

Ivy smiled, giggling softly, "Are you trying to ask me to dinner?"

Kursed nodded quickly, "Y-yeah, that is, if you want to."

She came up to him and lightly kissed his cheek, "I'd love to. When and where?"

He pulled away, clearing his throat, "My dorm, sometime in the evening."

Her eyes widened in interest, "Oh, you cook?"

He shuffled his feet, staring at the ground, "Kinda."

Ivy placed a hand under his chin, bringing him back to meet her eyes, "Are you bad at it?"

Kursed shook his head, "N-no, it's not that. It's just…I've never cooked for a…girl before."

Ivy giggled softly, "Well, I'm in the mood for chicken, baked, if you can handle it." She turned to leave, waving at him, "Later, Allen." She quickened her pace as she hurried for class.

Kursed stared after her, transfixed for a moment, before snapping out of it, "Oh no, now I'm even more late!" He sped off to class, ready for the strict lecture, followed by lines. He shuddered. Lines were the worst thing to do after doing homework, followed by studying. He smiled though, putting all those thoughts aside. He had a date tonight.

And her name was Ivy.

***

Kursed cried out as he accidentally cut himself from chopping vegetables, "Shoot!" He carefully placed the knife down on the cutting board, and turned his gaze toward the cut, blood oozing slightly. He stood there, transfixed upon the sight of his own blood trickling down. His stomach growled as if in response, as if begging for a taste. Licking his lips, he brought the finger up to his mouth, and began sucking on it. Oh, the taste! It was like wine against his tongue, making his mind grow fuzzy as he continued to suck on the wound.

His eyes snapped open, as he pulled the finger from his mouth, "What….what was that?" He shook his head, going over to the oven and checking on dinner. The chicken was a nice, golden brown color, the aroma making his stomach growl. He closed the oven and walked back to the board, finishing up the melody of vegetables.

There was a small knock on the door, alerting Kursed that his guest had arrived. Quickly, he dropped the vegetables into a simmering pot of water, and then headed for the door, opening it. There stood Ivy, smiling gently, "Hello there, Allen."

Kursed's eyes were wide as he took in her outfit. She wore tight, form-fitting black jeans that dared to show every curve. Her shirt was a black, tight tank top that left just enough for the imagination. Her hair and chest bounced as she sauntered inside, hips swaying from side to side. She sniffed the air lightly, "What's that delicious smell?"

Kursed took her black jacket from her arms, chuckling softly, "That would be dinner. Hungry, are we?"

She slipped up to him, eyes lustful, "Ravenous." Her lips met his as she started to lead him through the paces, hands exploring his chest and shoulders. Quickly, she bit his lip, snaking her tongue into his mouth, making him moan in response, as he tightened his grip around her body. She moved in closer, gently continuing to bite his lip. Pausing, she pulled away, sniffing, "Allen, what's burning?"

Kursed was puzzled at first, until his eyes widened, recognizing the smell, "The chicken!" He ran toward the kitchen area, peering through the haze of smoke. Grabbing an oven mitt, he threw open the door to see more smoke pour out. He pulled out the blackened bird, throwing it against the counter, "It's ruined!" He growled softly to himself, running a hand through his hair.

Ivy came up to him, sliding her arms around his waist, "What's wrong, Allen?"

Kursed turned around to look at Ivy, "Hey, I'm sorry, Ivy." He pulled out of her embrace, going back into the sitting area and grabbing the phone, "How about pizza?"

Ivy wrapped her slim fingers around the phone and pulled it out of his grip, throwing it across the room. She snaked an arm around his waist and pulled him close, catching his lips with hers, beginning the same, rhythmic pace she had started before. Kursed closed his eyes, feeling her run her hands through his hair.

She pulled away, smiling softly. Placing a pale, smooth hand on his shoulders, she pushed him back against a chair. Quickly, she straddled him, meeting his gaze, "There now. Relax. I'm not going to bite…hard."

Kursed chuckled, "So, you're into that kinda thing, are you?"

Ivy nodded, "What are you into?"

He gently placed a hand around the back of her neck, pulling her close, "You." Their lips met, softly, then drinking each other in. Kursed ran his hand through her hair, twisting it between his fingers.

Ivy pulled away, "Allen, I have something to tell you."

Kursed sighed, "Me too."

She smiled politely, "You first, it's polite."

He ran a hand through his hair, sighing softly, "Allen…is my middle name. My first name is Kursed."

She bit her lip, "Why did you lie about your name?"

Kursed chuckled slightly, "Come on, would you have had dinner with someone whose name was Kursed?"

She giggled softly, "I'm not like other girls." She nuzzled him, lips softly touching his own, teasing him, "Besides, Ivy's my nickname. My real name is Ivory."

"Ivory," Kursed chuckled, "Beautiful name for a beautiful lady." He pulled her back, holding her tightly against his body, hearing her emit a small moan.

She pulled back, a small smile upon her lips, "I've also got a little secret."

Kursed smiled, eyes twinkling, "A sccrct, huh? Tell me, I love secrets."

She giggled softly, "Close your eyes and I'll tell you."

He chuckled, "Lay it on me."

Ivory brushed her lips against his ear, gently nibbling on it, "Are you ready?" He nodded. Baring her fangs, she quickly licked a small, hot path over a pulsing vein, before sinking her fangs in deep to the hilt. Hot, delicious blood pumped into her eager mouth, pure, yet it had that kick most would die to taste. Kursed let out a small groan as a sharp pain jolted through his body, slowly turning to pleasure as she drank. After some time, she pulled away, licking the blood off her lips, yet they still looked like they were stained with crimson.

Kursed moaned, eyes hazy as he lifted a hand up to his neck, almost as if in a lethargic state, "What…what did you do to me?" He winced as he touched his neck, pulling away to see blood staining his hands.

She grinned, "I fed from you." Her eyes were narrowed in amusement, "Your blood was quite delicious, I must say." She leaned in toward his throat, slowly licking the oozing blood away, "I want more." She bent down and began sucking on the wound, holding his body still. She pulled back after a few minutes, eyes crimson, "Thank you, Kursed."

He tried to speak, but she shushed him, placing two, cold fingers against his lips, "Hush now, for I am about to make you an offer I think you can't refuse." Her eyes narrowed, "Life, or death. Choose wisely, though, for you can't go back once you do."

Kursed's lips trembled as a blinding, white-hot pain lashed through his body, making him cry out, eyes wide. Ivory still straddled him, expectant for his answer. He took in a shuddering, ragged breath as he let out one word.

"Life."

Ivory smiled, "Excellent."

Kursed's vision was fuzzy as he tried to focus his line of sight. Something wet and hot was pressed against his cold, numb lips. "Drink," She hissed, voice commanding, "Drink the elixir."

Kursed opened his mouth, catching a small drop or two. The taste was familiar, coppery and metallic in a way. He wanted to spit it out, to gag, but Ivory forced him to continue drinking. After a few minutes, she gave a hard yank, pulling away from Kursed. She smiled, licking the wound clean, and seeing the skin begin to pull itself back together to heal. She looked over at Kursed, "How was it?"

His eyes widened as he realized what he had been so eagerly feeding on, her blood. He coughed weakly, sputtering in shock, "Vampire!"

Ivory flicked a strand of black hair behind her shoulders, "You chose this life, not me."

Kursed narrowed his eyes, "But you forced me!"

"And I could have let you died, couldn't I?" Ivory snapped, shutting him up, "But no, I gave you a choice." She narrowed her eyes, "Now, relax, and let the venom take its course."

Kursed opened his mouth to say something, but cried out again, breathing hard. His eyeteeth started to ache, growing sharp within seconds. He threw his head back and howled, eyes wide. He could feel his nail pop and grow into small claws. Finally, he slumped over in his chair, breathing hard and ragged.

Ivory smirked, "There now. That wasn't so bad, was it?"

Kursed growled, "You…harpy witch!"

She giggled, "I've been called worse by men far more elegant." Her smirk widened, "Which reminds me, you'll need to feed, and soon."

Kursed shook his head, throat dry and sore, "Never."

"You don't have a choice!" Ivory snapped, "Either you feed or you die. Simple as that!"

He shook his head, crying out in anger. Quickly, he pushed Ivory off of his lap, running out the door, breathing hard as he tried to escape from her. Once outside, in the cool night air, he stopped, catching his breath. There was a dull pounding in his head, small at first, then steadily growing in intensity, like a gong going off in his head. He needed something, but what?

"Excuse me, are you alright?"

Kursed could barely see a thing. Everything was hazy and wavering. He panted, trying to get a glimpse of the speaker. Before him stood a small, pretty blond with hazel eyes, wearing a light blue jacket over ripped jeans. She gently placed a hand on his shoulder, "Are you alright?"

Oh, he could hear it, the young girls' heartbeat fluttering like a small bird, frightened, but unsure. Her eyes were wide as saucers, shining in the moonlight. And her blood, it called to him, singing as vitality in her veins. Kursed licked his lips, letting out a small growl of hunger, of lust. He reached out to her, tightly clutching her shoulder. He couldn't breathe, he couldn't even see straight.

The young girl started to help him up, worry in her eyes, "Let's get you up now."

Kursed kept his head down, shoulders heaving. He quickly lifted up his head, baring his fangs. The girl cried out, tried to flee, but Kursed clamped a hand over her mouth and pulled her close, biting deeply into her throat. Warm, soothing blood flowed into his hungry mouth, increasing as her heart continued to beat. He growled, twisting his head this way and that to catch most of the ruby liquid that breathed life. The girl let out a small cry before dropping her head.

Kursed pulled away, roaring in victory. He took a couple of breaths before his vision returned. His body froze as he looked down at the young girl, shock registering on his face.

Her throat and jugular were completely ripped out, exposing the meat and flesh within. Her eyes were wide and glassy, mouth opened in a silent scream. Blood oozed from the hole in her pale throat, along with several small cuts along her arms where he had gripped her. Kursed hadn't let a single drop escape him. Raising a shaky hand, he touched his face, feeling something slick on his cheeks.

Soft giggling caught his attention, making him turn around. There stood Ivory, clapping softly, "Not too bad for your first kill, Kursed."

Kursed snarled at her, "Shut it!" He turned to leave, to dispose of the body.

Ivory held up her hand, "Stop."

Kursed froze, feet planted firmly on the ground. His eyes went wide, "What's…what's happening to me?"

Ivory sauntered over to him, chuckling softly, "Good, little one." She lightly touched his cheek, nails brushing softly.

"What did you do to me?" Kursed snarled.

"It's simple, really," Ivory chuckled, eyes narrowed, "I sired you, therefore, any command I give, so long as my blood runs through your veins, must be obeyed. I can even reach across distances just to issue a command." She gently kissed his lips, tasting the blood on his breath, "Now, was it really so bad to feed?" She cast a look toward the body, "Wow, did a better job than I could." She turned to leave, "Come, we must leave."

He shot her a look, "Wait, why?"

She shot him an equal look, "To clean you up, first off. Second, it must look as if Kursed was never here, to keep hunters among others from hunting us down." The wind blew through her hair, "Come, now."

Kursed cast one last look at the girl, before wrenching his gaze away, following after his sire.

***

The night was cold as the two of them ran across rooftops, following the scent of fresh blood. Ivory skidded slightly, looking down over at a dance club. She let out a small noise, "Seems to me like there's a lot of fresh blood in there."

Kursed nodded, the wind blowing through his now silver hair, "So, does Xanatos want us to recruit some fresh blood?"

Ivory laughed, fangs glinting in the neon lights, "No, we're here to

82

feed, is all." She stood over the side, eyes narrowed, "Go in there and find someone. Preferably someone we can share."

He rolled his eyes, "Whatever."

Her tone grew dangerous, "Don't fail me, Kursed." She leapt off the building, blending into the night. Kursed, sighing, followed suit.

The music was loud, banging against his eardrums. His mouth watered as he took in all sorts of scents. Ivory was right, this was the place. Sighing, he stepped inside.

The club was bouncing, with bodies moving and rubbing against each other to the beat of a small band onstage. The music was raunchy, but nevertheless got people moving around. Kursed sniffed the air lightly. There was someone here, but they were different, neither vampire nor lycan. What was this person? The crowd parted slightly, giving him room to hone in. It was a girl.

This girl had long, midnight black hair that seemed to change colors with the strobe lights. She turned her gaze upon Kursed and froze, hazel eyes wide. Kursed smirked, maybe this night would be entertaining after all.

He came up to this girl, letting a small smile grace his lips, "Hey there."

The girl smiled, yet still tense, unsure, "Hey yourself."

Kursed chuckled softly, eyes twinkling, "What's a pretty girl like yourself doing in a dump like this?"

She shrugged, "I don't know. I like the music." She slipped off her stool and started to weave a path to the dance floor, "Come and dance, if you wanna know more." She winked, hips swaying.

Kursed chuckled, meeting her on the floor, taking one of her hands and spinning her, then catching her, "Can you keep up?"

She grinned, "Of course." She was pulled up close to him, dipped down, then pulled back up. Quickly, Kursed picked her up, then dropped her back onto the ground. Smiling, he pulled up one of her long, luscious legs and slid his hand up her calf.

He came in close, breath hot against the nape of her neck, "What's your name?"

She smirked, taking his hand, "Follow me outside and I'll tell you." Quickly, she pulled him along out the door.

Several figures were on them at once, silent as they came closer. A tall, muscular blond stepped forward, grey eyes hard, "Meagen! There you are!"

The girl rolled her eyes, sighing, "Yeah, so?"

A redhead stepped up to the male, red eyes twinkling, "I was just worried about you, kitten. I mean, I am supposed to care for you."

Meagen smiled her thanks, "Oh! Almost forgot!" She pulled Kursed over to her, eyes filled with excitement, "Thane, I know we told you we'd find you an apprentice? Well, I found you one!"

Kursed growled, eyes wide, "What?"

Meagen giggled, "You get to stay with me if you agree."

Kursed smiled up at Thane, holding out his hand, "The name's Kursed."

Thane took his hand, shaking it. "Thane," He growled.

***

Asuka sat up in her bed, eyes wide as Kursed finished up his tale. "Wow," She breathed, "So, you met Meagen and Thane a few nights after Ivory sired you?"

Kursed nodded, "Yeah. Thane was brutal at first." Thane hit Kursed hard on the arm, making him sputter in surprise, "But we've been great ever since."

Thane sighed, "I suppose it's my turn." He closed his eyes, "Where to begin?"

Chapter 12

Another scream pierced the night, echoing in the forest near the holy city. Thane's head shot up, alert, waiting for another scream. He closed his eyes, spreading out his senses. Being a primordial had its perks, and this was one of them.

Quick footsteps ran past the doorway of Thane's hideout. There was a pause, before the footsteps came back, showing a lithe, yet athletic young teen with light brown hair, hazel eyes wide, "Master! There you are!"

Thane pulled on his coat, shivering slightly with the cold, "Kyrre, what's going on?"

"There's been another attack!" Kyrre exclaimed, "Another victim, drained of blood! Jenova wants to see you as soon as possible!"

Thane nodded, "Right! Did you see who did it?"

Kyrre shook his head, "No. Any eyewitnesses who did say that all they saw was a shadowy figure, followed by a flash of flames."

Thane felt his heart freeze as his eyes widened. A flash of fire? Why did it sound so familiar? He shook his head, "Never mind the witnesses. Just start a search for whatever did this. If you come across the killer, don't hesitate to kill them."

Kyrre nodded, "Right!" He took off, running into the shadows of the forest.

Thane narrowed his eyes, "Be careful, kid." He closed his eyes, letting the shadows rise up around him, and pulling him inside. Once again, he felt the familiar prickly sensation as he traveled through the shadows. He could sense the kill straight ahead, the death calling to him like a keening bell.

Out of the shadows Thane came, stony grey eyes narrowed as he took in the scene. Ahead of him was a mangled body, throat ripped out to expose the windpipe and meat. Coming closer, Thane saw that it was a man, mouth open in a silent scream. The stench of death hung over him and a small, yet lithe girl.

The small girl spun around to look behind her, "Thane! Thank the Gods!"

"What have we got?" Thane asked.

Jenova gestured to the body, "Once again, drained of blood, made to look like a wild animal got to them."

His eyes narrowed, "Looks like someone roughed him up a bit." He took in the sight again. A multitude of cuts appeared on the victims' face and body, along with several gashes, scabbing over. The neck looked broken, head turned on his side.

Jenova shivered slightly, "Horrid, isn't it?"

Thane didn't look at her, but to the forest, "Kyrre's out there looking for any evidence linking the killer to the crime."

Her jewel green eyes widened, remembering a time when Kyrre had entered the forest once, and hadn't returned. She bit her lip, "Are...are you sure that's...wise?"

Thane sighed, "Don't ask questions about what I don't have the answers to." He bowed his head. Maybe he should bring Kyrre back, leave him with Jenova, and go after the heartless killer himself. He could probably catch this killer faster than anyone, and make sure they suffered. And he even had the shadows on his side. Another perk of being a primordial, he supposed. He started for the forest, when Jenova called him back.

"Thane, wait!" She fidgeted, avoiding his hard gaze, "In all honestly, do you think Kyrre is safe?"

Thane looked toward the body, sensing power from the victim, but not much, must have been a mage. He looked back at Jenova, "In all honesty, I haven't the foggiest. We can only hope."

Her eyes were wide as she continued to bite her lip, "Please, Thane, bring Kyrre back, safe and sound."

He nodded, "I'll do my best." Closing his eyes, he let his body merge with the darkness, feeling his body being pulled forward. Another loud, keening cry could be heard nearby. Thane wrenched himself from the shadows, near another part of town. There was a muffled, gurgling sound close by. He paused, breath silent, keeping his eyes open.

There was a shadowy blur as something sped past him. Thane whirled around, eyed wide "What was that?" There was a muffled scream, close by his position. He ran forward, following the muffled sounds. He turned the corner and froze, taking in the sight before him.

In the shadows of a building area was a hunched figure, bent over at the throat of a struggling man. A pale, slim hand was covering his mouth, making him whimper. Thane took a cautious step forward, keeping a slim dagger under his sleeve, while holding his breath. He took another step, creeping closer. Silently, he let the dagger slip down his arm, the handle resting tightly in his grip. Slowly, he brought it up as he took another step closer.

The hunched figure paused, the ravenous slurping noises stopping as she released the man, letting him hit the ground hard. It stood up, locking crimson red eyes with Thane. This figure wore a black robe, face concealed by a hood. A slim hand reached up, pulling the hood away, revealing a young woman. She had long, raven black hair and crimson red eyes. Her skin shown in the moonlight, almost giving her an aura of sorts. She smiled, fangs glinting in the light, "Put the dagger away, mortal, I won't hurt you."

Thane's grip on the dagger tightened as he narrowed his eyes, "I'm not a mortal, and obviously you're not either."

The woman laughed, making Thane jump slightly. He silently cursed himself for that one, "What gave me away? Was it my aura, shadow boy, or perhaps it was my fangs, no?"

Thane took another step back, feeling her eyes bore into his own, "I wouldn't suggest fighting me, boy. I am a mind reader, after all." She hissed, a small smile played upon her lips, "In fact, even though you're hiding it, you're unsure about me. There's also a bit of fear there, laying within." She smiled, "Also, there's a face that keeps coming to mind." She giggled, "He's cute, I'll give him that. Maybe I'll go after him next."

Thane felt a surge of anger rise within him as a shadowy tendril lashed forward, wrapping around her throat and pinning her to the ground. "You ever go near him, I'll kill you faster than I've ever killed anyone."

She laughed, "What's he to you, huh? A brother, a lover? Come on, I'm dying to hear this!" She giggled at her own pun, "Dying, get it?" She let her body merge into the shadows, escaping his grip.

Thane blinked in surprise. Narrowing his eyes, he growled, "Where are you? Show yourself!"

The woman giggled, the sound echoing all around him, "Later, shadow boy. We'll meet again, I promise."

Thane sighed. Well, no flash of fire. She there must be two killers. God, he was so tired. He was getting too old for meaningless hunts like this. Whoever that girl was, though, she was dangerous, and needed to be put down. Turning around, he started the slow trek back, taking his time to think, let his mind wander for once. A small rustling sound near the trees made Thane pause, body tense and ready for action if needed.

Out of the shadows came Kyrre, who had a few leaves here and there in his hair from the branches. He looked up at Thane, eyes wide, "Master!"

Thane quickly pulled Kyrre over to him, checking his throat and shoulders for marks, "Good, you're alright."

Kyrre nodded, "Yeah, but I heard noises, so I decided to check it out." His eyes remained wide, "Have you found the killer?"

Thane hesitated, unsure of how to put the encounter to words, "Look, kid, go back to Jenova and stay with her."

Kyrre shook his head, "I want to go find the killer, too!"

Thane narrowed his eyes, "You're not ready to face the killer. Not yet." He pinched the bridge of his nose, "I don't even know if I'm ready." He sighed, "Go back to Jenova, she's worried about you."

Kyrre bowed his head, knowing there was no arguing with Thane, "Alright." He lifted his head up, eyes narrowed and full of resolution, "Be safe, Master."

Thane nodded, "Don't dawdle. Go straight back to the city." Kyrre nodded, then took off.

Thane let out another soft sigh, time to hunt down the killer. He kept his eyes open and alert as he spread out his senses through the shadows, searching for anyone or anything. There was someone there, and whoever it was, was close.

"Thane?"

He paused. *No,* He thought, *That voice. Couldn't be.* He went to turn around, to see who spoke his name.

Two slim and pale arms wrapped around his waist, sliding up his chest the way his old love used to do. "Please," The voice begged, "Don't turn around. Not just yet." She chuckled softly, "Just…let me hold you, the way I used to."

That voice, it was so familiar. Slowly, he turned around and stood face to face with a fiery redhead, her emerald green eyes wide as she painted a small smile upon her lips. "Alena," Thane whispered, eyes wide with disbelief, "No. I…I don't believe it."

She laughed softly, "It's me, Thane. I'm here to stay."

He shook his head, backing away from her, "You died. I saw you die."

She bit her lip, "I was saved, Thane, and given a new life." She shook her head, "Look, I know what I've done before was wrong, and I've accepted that, but I want to change, starting now." She reached out for his hand, her touch cool, "Please, let's go for a drink, on me."

Thane narrowed his eyes, "Try anything at all, and I'll kill you for good this time."

She chuckled, "Same old Thane. Come on."

He hesitated at first, thinking about that encounter with that strange woman, but then shook it off as Alena pulled him ahead. She leaned her head on his shoulder, smiling, "Oh, how I've missed you."

Thane nodded, "I've missed you, too."

She stopped in front of a pub, pulling open the door, "After you." He stepped inside, throat feeling thick from the hazy smoke in the air, mingled with the taste of whiskey and vodka in the air. Here and there were groups huddled together, while several sat at the bar, laughing away at crude jokes while sucking down shots.

Alena sauntered forward, eyes narrowed in amusement. She took a seat down over at the bar, tapping the counter softly, "I'll have whatever's the strongest here."

Thane sat next to her, "I'll take the same." The bar wrench nodded, then hustled away, preparing their drinks.

Alena looked over at Thane, red lips curved in a ghost of a smile, "My master and I watched your fights with Axis. You were brilliant."

Thane nodded to the serving wrench as she placed down their drinks, the strong smell hitting his senses, "Really?" He tipped the glass to his lips, drinking deeply, the mix of alcohol burning through his body, "And why didn't you help?"

Alena shrugged, "Master said it was none of our concern, so why bother?"

"We could have used your help," Thane said, refusing to look at her.

She chuckled, "After coming back, I had no idea if I could use my powers." She nodded to his drink, "Drink up, Thane, I want to head to the forest after this."

Thane shook his head, "I'm not really that thirsty."

She placed a hand on his, "Please, Thane, I really don't want to stay here much longer." She looked up at the young, hunched over server, who kept her head down and out of sight.

Thane shrugged, "Sure, if you want that." He took another swig, coughing slightly and making a face.

Alena laughed, "You've changed a bit, Thane."

He looked at her, puzzlement in his eyes, "How so?"

She lifted a finger and started to run it along the rim of her glass, "You used to be tough as nails, and killed others for profit. Now you've befriended others, and created unbreakable bonds."

"I still kill," Thane said, taking another drink.

She shook her head, "Not so much, though, Thane" Alena smiled softly, "I guess war does change a person."

He nodded, finishing his drink, "Yeah."

She smiled, taking his hand, "Come on, let's go. I've been getting strange stares since we've been here, and it's really making me uncomfortable." She pulled him along, trying to head for the exit.

A drunken stranger reached out, smacking her behind. "Hey sexy," He whistled, slurring his words, "Why don't you come party with me for awhile? You look like a party girl."

Thane stepped forward, feeling anger rise within him, but Alena stepped forward, smiling at the stranger. Slowly, she placed a hand under his chin, giggling softly, "Why don't you come with us outside, big boy? We're taking the party out there."

He grinned stupidly, sliding off his stool, "Alright, let's have ourselves a party!"

Alena grinned coyly, walking back over to Thane, "Follow us, handsome." The drunkard nodded like a doofus, following behind them.

Once outside, Alena turned around, eyes flashing, "Now, stand still and don't say a word, alright?" The stranger nodded. Alena smiled, "I've got a surprise for you, so be a good boy and close your eyes."

He laughed, "Okay!" He closed his eyes, lips puckered, waiting for a kiss.

Alena stared at him for a moment, before closing her eyes. A split second later, she threw them open, eyes red as flames. Fire started by the strangers' feet, before rushing up, licking his body. He started to cry out, twisting this way and that to try and put the flames out, before finally falling to the ground, letting the flames take him.

Thane shook his head, too horrified to speak. This was not his Alena. This was a monster in sheep's' clothing. His eyes hardened, "Why did you do that?"

She growled, "He was scum, so I put him where he belonged." Her eyes flashed dangerously, "Do you want to be next?"

Thane growled, pulling out a blade from his belt and tossed it at Alena, who just stood there, unmoving.

Quickly, she sidestepped to the right and kicked him hard in the small of his back. He sprawled out onto the grass near the forest, the air whooshing out of him in a rush. He tried to get up, but his sight began to blur, "What's this?" He asked himself, "What's…wrong with me?" He thought for a moment, then, "The drink! There must have been something in the drink!"

Alena sauntered up to him, placing a hand under his chin, "Yes, there was something in your drink." She smiled, "Something my master told me about. It's a simple little toxin that's tasteless, colorless, and odorless. It activates with fresh air, which is why it didn't do anything at first. What you're feeling is temporary. The effects will wear off after awhile." She slowly licked her lips, "But not until I've finished with you."

She snapped her fingers, which caused fire to rise up, spreading around Thane and enclosing him in a complete circle. His eyes widened, as her face glowed in the firelight. Emerald eyes glittered with hatred. Alena stepped forward, the smile on her face turning slowly into a scowl, "Why fight me on this? Why fight your old love?"

Thane gritted his teeth, "I don't want to fight anyone anymore, Alena!" He shook his head, vision blurring in and out, "Alena, tell me, what happened to the girl I used to know?"

Alena snarled, eyes wide with rage, "You killed her!" Her chest heaved up and down as she was breathing hard, glaring at him, "You ripped out her heart and killed her!" She smiled, "Which is why I'm going to pass this curse onto you."

Thane shook his head, "No deal, Alena. And when I get over there, I'm going to slit your throat and watch the light fade from your eyes."

The flames roared higher around him, almost searing his skin. Alena shook her head, "I would suggest not fighting me on this, Thane." She pulled out a small, slim dagger from her boot, "If you will not cooperate, then I guess I'll have no choice." She brought it up.

Thane's eyes widened, remembering a similar time when she had stabbed herself before, in his own arms, no less. He reached out to her, "Alena, no!" She brought it down toward her midsection, hissing in pain as her eyes went wide. Slowly, she fell to her knees, crimson staining the front of her shirt and hands. The flames vanished, leaving absolutely no traces around Thane. He ran forward, eyes wide, "Alena, please don't be dead! Come on!"

Her eyelids fluttered open as her breathing was ragged, "Help me up...please, Thane."

He gently slid an arm around her back, near her waist, the other behind her neck, and gently lifted her up, "Alena, why?"

Her lips parted as she tried to speak. She pulled herself closer to him, eyes half-open, "For this.' She rushed forward, throwing her arms around his neck, pulling him close. Snarling, she quickly sank her fangs deep into his throat.

Thane's eyes widened as he tried to pull away, the pain burning through his body. He continued to struggle, to pull away, but Alena held on tightly, unmoving. Suddenly, the pain stopped, turning into pleasure as she nursed from the wound, making him throw his head back, emitting a small little noise. He closed his eyes, his vision starting to blur completely. After a few minutes, as far as he could tell, she let go.

Alena brought up the dagger she had used, and sliced deep into her wrist. She brought it over to Thane's lips. "Drink," She commanded.

He shook his head, pushing her away, "No, I won't do it."

She growled, grabbing the hair on the back of his head, "Do it, Thane. Otherwise, you'll die."

He shook his head again, "No, I won't."

Alena gritted her teeth, eyes narrowed. She thrust the wrist forward, pressing it against his cold lips, "If you will not drink, I will make you." Her gaze hardened, "Now, drink."

Thane tried to struggle, but the drug and the blood loss made his mind swim. Suddenly, blinding white pain lashed through him, making him cry out. Spasms rocked through his body as he tried to speak. He threw his head back, crying out, feeling like multiple daggers were being thrust through his body, "Alena...what's...what's happening to me?"

Alena brought his head up, the blood oozing a tiny bit off of her wrist, "Drink Thane. The pain will go away if you do." She brought up her wrist, "Please, Thane." She pressed it against his lips.

His mouth parted, the blood flowing inside his mouth. Slowly, his eyes closed as he took another swallow, then another. Part of him wanted to gag, to spit out the metallic taste. But another part of him wanted to pull the wrist closer, to get more of that elixir that was like wine on his tongue. He could feel some of the pain receding as he drank.

Finally, Alena pulled her wrist away, binding it, "So, how do you feel, Thane?"

Thane slowly opened his eyes, clenching and unclenching his fists. The pain was throbbing slightly, no longer a hindrance. He looked over at Alena, eyes narrowed, "W-why did you do this to me?" He got up and started to leave.

Alena followed behind him, "You can't go back to the others now."

"Watch me," He growled, hurrying back to the city.

Alena narrowed her eyes, "You're a blind fool. But you will learn, one way or another." Her eyes flashed red.

Thane ignored her and continued on. His head pounded while his stomach growled. He should have killed her when she first spoke his name. None of this would have happened if he had. He shook his head, no, he couldn't have killed her. Sure, he had loved her once, and was hurt when she had betrayed his loyalty for Axis. And when they had fought it out, he went easy on her, because a part of him still loved her twisted self. He growled, nothing was making sense.

Thane made it through the clearing near the holy city. His vision was hazy as he tried to see. He took a shaky step forward, then another, before falling to the ground. God, he was so weak. He shouldn't feel this way, the toxin should have worn off by now. So what was causing it now? His mouth began to hurt as something sharp thrust through his gums, making them ache. He tried to get up, but failed.

"Thane! Are you alright?"

Two slim hands gently gripped his shoulders, helping him up. Thane looked through his blurred vision to see Jenova next to him, green eyes wide with fright, "You're so cold. Come on, let's get you inside and warm you up."

He reached out to her, gripping her shoulder tightly, "No, Jenova, I can't."

Her eyes narrowed in puzzlement, "Thane, are you alright?" She helped him sit up.

His shoulders heaved as her next words began to trail off, no longer registering in his head. All he could hear was a soft, pounding noise, compared to the gong in his head. A small, flowery smell was in the air, close by. Thane looked over at Jenova, smiling softly, "Hey, listen, thanks for looking after Kyrre for me, all this time."

Jenova's face colored slightly, "Thanks….I think."

He pulled himself up, meeting her gaze, "You're a wonderful girl Jenova, which is why your blood's so pure."

She blinked in confusion, "Huh? What are you getting at?"

He chuckled, gaze never leaving her own, "I'm just proud of you, is all." He got closer to her, "Thank you." He wrapped her arms around the small girl, and swiftly bit deep into her throat.

She let out a small, startled cry, then relaxed, eyelids fluttering. The blood flowed into his mouth as he slowly drank from the wound. It was hot, yet it had a bit of a smaller taste to it. The girl was brave, especially coming out to him in the state he was in. But, she was also afraid. Her body shook against his own as he bit deeper. She tried to pull away, but Thane held her close, trying to get at the ruby liquid he needed to make the pain go away.

After awhile, he let her go, letting her fall to the ground. Thane licked his lips, vision returning to normal. He looked down and sucked in a breath. Jenova lay with her head tilted to one side, eyes wide and glazing over with death, her skin pale, while her throat had been ripped out, leaving no traces of blood in her body. He tried to speak, but no sound came out.

Alena came up behind him, eyes narrowed with pride, "Not bad for your first kill."

Thane growled, eyes wide with anger, "Shut it, Alena!"

Alena laughed, "I must say, you did her nicely. Well done."

He refused to look at her, "Best look your fill, because I swear, I'll never harm another innocent again."

Her eyes narrowed, "You are a predator, just like a wolf or a shark. You've had a taste of it, and you'll taste it again." She smiled, lips dripping with poison, "You can run, but you can never hide from your hunger." She beckoned to him, "Come, we must leave now."

Thane shook his head, "Never." He turned to leave.

"Stop."

The command rang through the night, clear as bells. He threw a hard gaze back at her, "What is this?"

Alena smiled, "I sired you. My blood runs through your veins. Whatever command I give must be obeyed, even if I gave you a command before I died, it must be obeyed." She turned to leave, "Come, the body will soon be discovered. We must flee, or hunters will come."

Thane cast a final look at Jenova, before taking off, following after Alena.

***

Asuka let out a small noise, eyes wide, "Oh, wow, Thane."

Thane shook his head, "Just wait. There's more."

Chapter 13

Thane sat at a rather large piano, playing an old tune his love used to sing back in the good old days. He had loved Alena, but also one other. One with a kind and gentle soul who would have been appalled at killing someone, or even watching Thane kill someone. A small flurry of emotion rose within him, but playing the piano helped soothe the animal within him, the animal Alena had brought out.

There was soft laughter near the door. Alena must have brought back a stooge or two using her newfound charm. He rolled his eyes as she led in two girls, smelling of nothing but drink. There was a blonde who seems to have had more than her friend. She kept casting lustful looks over at Thane, batting her eyelashes and smiling. Thane shook his head, going back to the piano, feeling the bloodlust rise slowly within him.

Alena gestured to Thane, smiling softly, "Ladies, this is my friend, Thane. Thane, say hello."

He threw a cold look over at the girls, nodding curtly. The blonde came over to toward him, sitting beside him on the seat, "Why so cold, love?"

Alena laughed, the small brunette beside her giggling softly, "Thane's just a cold fish. He needs a proper lady to bring him out of his shell." She turned back to the brunette, sitting down next to a small fireplace and patting the spot next to her, "Now, you come here. Come share your secrets with me."

Thane shook his head in disgust. Alena sure knew how to throw herself onto others. The blonde scooted over to him, ocean blue eyes wide with amusement and lust, "So, are you shy, Thane?"

Thane shook his head "No, I'm not." The pounding in his head returned, faint at first, then slowly growing in intensity. He would have to feed again, and his next prey was right next to him. His vision blurred slightly as he tried to speak. He looked over at Alena, who was giggling softly with the brunette.

The blonde brought his gaze back, smiling as she gently pressed her lips against his own. Emitting a small growl, he snaked an arm around the wrench's' waist and brought her close to him, pinning her against the piano while she ran her fingers through his hair.

He pulled back for a moment, the pounding in his head still growing, deafening him, "Tell me, what's your name?"

She giggled, bringing her lips toward his ear, "Anna Maria."

"Beautiful name," He gently kissed her lips again, making her giggles as he did so. She leaned more against the piano, shoulders heaving up and down. He bent toward her ear, gently nibbling on it, "Close your eyes, pretty one." She did so, feeling him trace kisses down to her throat. He slowly kissed a pulsing vein, as his mind screamed with pain. Holding the back of her neck with a free hand, he sank his fangs deep into the hilt, tasting the richness that always made his headaches vanish.

She cried out at first, tried to pull away, but Thane growled, holding onto her and biting deeper. Another loud cry rang through his ears, knowing that Alena had gotten the brunette to trust her long enough to taste her. His grip tightened around on the back of the blondes' neck, as he drank deeper, trying to get at the ruby liquid that spoke life and sung with vitality. Blood pumped forth, some landing on the keys of the piano.

The blonde gurgled slightly, before sighing, eyes wide open. He pulled away after a few moments, feeling his headache slowly ebb away while his sight returned. The blonde was slumped over the keys, motionless scrap meat. Thane closed his eyes as his mind returned to him. He always got like this after a kill, regret and sorrow in his heart. He was tired of killing, of blacking out and saying things he would not mean just to get what he wanted.

Alena came up behind him, pulling his face over to hers and softly kissing him, tasting the fresh kill upon his lips, "Better?"

Thane nodded, "A bit." He walked over to the small table near the fireplace and sat beside it, eyes narrowed as if in thought.

Alena smiled at him, "I'm going to dispose of these two." She gently kissed his cheek, "When I come back, please tell me what's bothering you." She turned to leave.

Thane knew what was bothering him, being a killer. He was a killer before, but even that got old, started to lose its touch. He never asked to be a vampire, but was forced into it. His mind thought back to his other love, his goddess. Why did she have to leave him, why did she have to die? He missed her terribly, as he had hidden her gift to him. The book with his victims' names written inside was hidden away, as it reminded him of her.

Footsteps came up behind him, gently wrapping her arms around his shoulders. For one absurd moment, Thane thought it was his goddess, returning once more from the dead. Alena chuckled softly, "Tell me, what's wrong, Thane?"

He turned around, looking away, "Tell me, Alena, I want to know about these headaches I get before I feed, among other things."

She smiled, "I see what you mean, the headaches first. It's to let you know when you have to feed, otherwise, you'll attack out of blind need."

"That explains what happens after I've feed," Thane muttered, "What about passion and bloodlust? What's all that about?"

Alena sighed, "Nosy little one, aren't you?" She giggled softly, "Passion and pain are intense with our kind. In fact, any sensation is intense. Be it passion, pleasure, or pain."

"So, when you stabbed yourself the night I was sired, it really did hurt?" Thane asked.

She nodded, "Not everything that night was a trick. It we get hurt and start bleeding, we can die, unless we feed."

"Namely me," Thane said, "You got me out of revenge."

Alena nodded, "That, and because I wanted you. Your blood was quite lovely, very filling." She locked eyes with his, seeing a mingling of emotions, "You're still hungry, aren't you?"

Thane shook his head, "The headache's barely there."

She shook her head, "The venom won't affect me, and I can sense your pain." She moved stray hairs away from her pale throat, "Do it, you won't hurt me."

He gently slid a hand around the nape of her neck, kissing the spot, before biting down, slowly drinking in the blood, the taste slightly sweeter, like rich wine coating his tongue. In his minds' eye, he saw faded memories, memories of the two of them, followed by mingled emotions. He pulled back, hardly breathing.

Alena let out a small breath, the smile returning to her face, "There now, better?"

Thane nodded, "Much." He pulled her back, softly licking away the blood as the wound began to heal. She laid her head against his shoulder, slowly closing her eyes.

She snuggled against Thane, quiet for a moment, then, "Thane, do you think we're on the wrong side?"

Thane looked down at her, eyes filled with puzzlement, "What brought this on all of a sudden?"

Alena turned her gaze up to him, "Being near Xanatos is well, disturbing. He's starting to get more bloodthirsty, and keeps all sorts of slaves and playthings at his disposal." She shook her head, "He told me he wants us back at his palace with him. Oddly enough, though, he really wants you, says you'll be his perfect little weapon." She chuckled softly, "As if I'd let him have you, you're mine."

Thane growled, "I don't belong to anyone." Alena didn't answer him at first, body stiff. He gently shook her, trying to get her attention, "Alena, you okay?"

Her eyes went wide as she hardly breathed, "Thane, my master is coming!" She jumped up, trying to think.

Thane bolted after her, "Alena, what's going on?"

Her fearful eyes met his as she tried to speak, "My master and Xanatos are tired of waiting for us. So I've been given an order, surrender or die."

"That's absurd!" Thane exclaimed, "I'll fight your master! We can take him!"

"Her," She corrected, "My master is a woman. And no, I can't lose you." She bit her lip, "If I say hide, you hide, and to run, you run. Got it?" He didn't say anything at first. Her gaze hardened, "Answer me!"

He nodded, "Got it."

She froze again, body ridged, "Hide, now!"

"What about you?" Thane asked.

She bit her lip, looking down, "She's given me another order. I am to stay and meet her, and I cannot use my powers." She smiled gently, "Last time I disobeyed, I got lashed with their silver whips." She shoved him, "Get going!"

He took off into the other room and hid under the bed, hearing voices, unsure of who they belonged to.

"Where is he?"

"He took off, ran for it."

"Liar."

There was a smacking sound as Alena cried out, "He did! I swear it! He sensed danger and fled!"

"You're lying, and I know it. Now tell me where he is!"

Alena ran into the room Thane was hiding in, followed by a woman whose boots clunked where she walked, slowly stalking Alena, "You're lying. Tell me, now!"

"No!" There was a scuffling sound as the woman lunged forward. Thane heard several more shrieks and grunts of pain until Alena was thrown to the ground.

The woman straddled her, chuckling softly, "Now, tell me, pretty Alena."

Alena shook her head, "Never!" She struggled.

The woman pulled out a knife and quickly stabbed Alena's side. Alena refused to cry out as the woman slowly pulled it out, "You know he belongs to Xanatos. Now, look at me."

Alena cast a look toward Thane, before looking back at the woman, "The closet. He's in the closet."

The woman seemed satisfied as she got up from Alena, walking over to the closet. Alena looked back at Thane, sending him a mental message, *Go.*

Thane slowly shook his head, *Not without you.*

The woman slammed the door shut, then walked back toward Alena, "You're lying. Look at me." Her voice dropped a bit, almost like a soft hiss.

Alena closed her eyes, looking away from her. A pale, slim hand forced her head back to her, "Look, Alena, and tell me where he is."

Alena's eyes snapped open as she stared back at the woman, "He's under the bed."

She had sold him out. The woman dropped to her knees, red eyes searching.

There was no one there.

Growling, the woman brought out her knife again and stabbed Alena repeatedly with it, laughing as Alena shrieked in pain. Finally, strong hands reached down and wrapped around Alena's slim neck, tightening their grip, then breaking her neck, a single, loud crack in the air. Satisfied, the woman left the room, searching.

Thane materialized from the shadows, crawling out onto his stomach to get to Alena. He cast a final look at her, before hearing a voice in his head.

Go.

He shook his head, he had to leave. Quickly, while the womans' back was turned, he darted quickly outside, leaving the door wide open. He put on a bust of speed as he fled for the shadows, his sanctuary. Footsteps followed after him, but he didn't stop, didn't look back.

There was a whoosh of air, followed by a sharp pain. Something stabbed the small of his back, bringing him down. He tried once, twice to use the shadows for protection, but he couldn't even move his arms. There was a loud gong going off in his head as his vision began to swim. Clanking footsteps alerted him to someones' presence, someone who came prepared. He tried to get up, but his body felt like lead.

A raven-haired beauty came over to him, rolling him over, "Hello, little one."

He tried to speak, "A-and what do y-you want with m-m-me?"

"A deal," She knelt beside him, "Join us, or we start killing."

Thane shook his head, "Never."

The woman laughed, "Bring him out, boys."

The dark creatures hiding in the shadows brought out a lean, athletic-built teen from the shadows. The boys' eyes widened, "Master!"

"Kyrre!" Thane sat up, head swimming more and more, "Hold on!" He tried to concentrate, to bring the shadows forward.

The woman laughed, "Hold it." She walked over to Kyrre, "He's part of the deal."

Thane growled, "What do you want?"

The woman laughed, "As I said, I want you to join us, and I will let the boy go." She gently kissed Kyrre's cheek, taking in his scent, "So delicious, makes me pretty hungry."

Thane tried to move, but arms fell down upon him, pinning him down, "Let him go!"

The woman giggled, "Only if you join us." She brought out her knife, "Otherwise, we'll have to remove some things from Kyrre." She brought the knife up to his nose, "Maybe snip off his nose, give him a smaller one? Or perhaps I should slowly gorge out his eyes, he doesn't need them anyways. Then I'll slice off his tongue, boys should learn to be quieter. Either way, the more you resist, the more painful it will be for him." She brought her lips over to his throat, baring her fangs as she slowly slid them through Kyrre's skin.

Kyrre cried out as the woman bit harder, holding him tightly. Thane felt his heart wrench everytime Kyrre cried out. He growled, "Enough!"

The woman let go of Kyrre, eyes a brighter shade of red then before, "What did you say?"

Thane sighed, "I'll join, just let Kyrre go."

Kyrre's eyes went wide, "Master, no!"

The woman threw him aside, striding over to Thane, and gripping the back of his head tightly "Say…it…again," She hissed, voice low, "I want to hear you hiss it like the lowly little snake you are."

Thane glared at her, breathing hard, "I'll join you, just let Kyrre go."

The woman smiled, "Excellent." She turned her gaze to the surrounding demons, "There's no reason to keep the boy, dig in!"

Thane's eyes widened, reaching out to Kyrre, who was already writhing, "No, Kyrre, no!"

A sharp, stabbing jab poked Thane's back, injecting a cool liquid within his system. His head swam as he fell to the ground, body shaking with anger and cold. He could smell the fear wafting off Kyrre in waves. The kid should have run, but he didn't. Thane tried to get up, tried to smash the demons that held onto him, tried to struggle and fight, but fell forward. The last thing he saw before blacking out, was a head coming off, blood splattering everywhere, and the demons roaring in victory as they held up their trophy.

***

Thane awoke, head throbbing as he tried to see. He cleared his throat, "Where am I?" He tried to bring his hand up, but felt something restrain him.

Soft laughter echoed around him as the young woman from before stepped out from the shadows, syringe in hand. Inside the syringe was a clear liquid that radiated with a slight aura. "Reinforced steel," The woman said, "Not even vampires can break them. Believe me, I've tried."

Thane bared his fangs, mouth dry as cotton, "What's with the needle?"

The woman laughed, "Xanatos has given orders to inject you with lycan venom. You are to receive the honor of becoming the first hybrid." She drew closer, lips dripping with poison.

Thane growled, "Torture me all you want. I'm not about to become your tool."

The woman laughed softly, "I'm afraid you have no choice." Her eyes narrowed, "You're locked up in one of our little toys, weak as a kitten." She scowled, "Doesn't mean we can't play first." She brought up her clawed hand and slowly dragged them over his chest, leaving marks and bleeding trails in her wake.

She brought up a bloody claw, slowly licking it off, "Your blood's quite delicious. Shame your sire wouldn't let us have you. Oh well." She swiftly jabbed the needle into his arm, depressing the plunger.

Thane cried out as white-hot pain lashed through him. He tried to struggle against his bonds, but it only continued to zap his strength.

The vampire smiled at him, "Rest now, a meal will be brought to you shortly." She stepped out the barred door, leaving it unlocked.

Thane's body shook as his mind screamed. He could feel the hunger rise within him. Sweat broke out on his head. God, he needed to feed, as soon as possible. He tried again with the bonds, tried to materialize with the shadows, but he was so weak.

The door opened again, the vampire throwing in a small figure, "Bon appetite." She pressed a switch on the wall, and then slammed the door, locking it.

There was a small squeak of noise as the figure jumped up and started pounding on the door, "Lemme out! Please! Someone, lemme out!"

Thane felt his bonds open, releasing him from the torture device. He slumped to the floor, breathing hard as his vision went in and out. The girls' cries were drowned out by the pounding in his head. All he could hear among that was a small, fluttering heartbeat, fluttering with fear. Her blood sung to him, singing with vitality. His mouth ached as his fangs slid down.

He cleared his throat, "Excuse me."

The young girl squeaked again, eyes wide, "Oh no!"

He came closer to her, "Why so afraid?"

The small girl pressed herself against the door, eyes never leaving his, "Are you one of those bad men here to kill me?"

Thane shook his head, "I'm not one of them." He came closer. He just had to calm her, to ease her mind. Oh, how he needed her blood. She wouldn't mind. He gripped her shoulders in an iron grip.

The girl cried out, feeling his hot breath against her slim neck. She scrunched up her eyes, body tense, "No, please!"

Thane paused, inches away from her throat. Slowly, he pulled away, eyes filled with puzzlement, "Jenova?"

The girl gave him a look, "Who?"

He shook his head, "Never mind." He cast a gentle look toward the girl, "Say, how would you like to get out of here?"

Her eyes widened, "Really?"

Thane shakily got up, smiling softly, "Yeah, I'm strong enough to bust us out of here."

She smiled, "Goody!" She ran forward and hugged him, "Thank you! Thank you so much!"

Thane gave her a curious look, "Answer me one thing, though."

She nodded, "Anything."

He grew serious, "What's a child like you doing here?"

She licked her dry lips, "Well, Xanatos used to know my parents, and he murdered them when he found out they were about to join the rebels." She lowered her gaze, "I was one of his little slaves, bleeding for his enjoyment."

Thane growled. He hated the man already. Who goes around using children as slaves? He shook his head, "Okay, listen, and listen well. I'm going to break through this door, and I want you to run. Distract the guards, I'll be behind you, killing them. You understand?" She nodded, "Good. Now stand back, and watch a master in action."

He closed his eyes, reaching out to the power he needed to give him strength, to protect. Shadowy dark tendrils rose up, snaking into the air. His eyes snapped open, directing them toward the door. There was a loud crack in the air as the door blasted open, hanging off its' hinges.

He gestured over to the door, nodding at the small girl, "Go on. I'll be right behind you. Trust me."

She nodded, "I trust you." She winked, "Wish me luck!"

Thane stuck to the shadows, watching as the small child ran past the guards, giggling softly, "Come get me, come get me!" The child was smart, knew how to evade the creatures. Thane quickly snuck up behind each and everyone, leading the shadows forward, and suffocating each and every one of them.

The girl waved at him, just up ahead, "Hey, I found an exit! Let's go!" She ran through a small opening, giggling softly. Thane ran to the opening, cool air hitting his face. Closing his eyes, he leapt through the hole, and fell down the cliff face, hitting almost every stone and bump he could. Finally, he landed hard beside the small child, who was holding her ankle.

He came over to the small child, eyes gentle, "You okay?"

She nodded, "Yeah. I think I sprained my ankle, though."

"Let me look at it," Thane gently lifted up her pant leg to see a slight discoloration on her ankle, along with some swelling. He nodded, "Luckily it's all you got." He scrunched up his eyes in pain as he fell to the ground.

The girl knelt beside him, eyes wide, "Hey, are you alright?"

Thane groaned, "Y-yeah. Just a little tired and sore, is all." He knew what he needed, he just refused to take it from the girl.

The girl nodded, as if in understanding, "You're one of those people who need blood. Please, take it from me."

He shook his head, "No, I won't."

The girl moved stray hairs away from her slim throat, "Please, you saved me. Now I'm saving you."

Thane slid a hand behind her neck, "One more question, though. What's your name?" He licked his lips, closing his eyes so he wouldn't see what he was about to do.

"Lilan," She breathed.

"Thane," He said, quickly sinking his fangs into her pale throat. He drank deeply, the pain in his body receding as relief flooded in. Lilan let out a small cry before letting her head fall forward.

Thane pulled away from her throat, red staining his lips, "Lilan?" He gently shook the girl, "Come on, little one, you gotta wake up." She didn't stir. His eyes widened, "Lilan?" Remembering what Alena did to save him, he quickly bit deep into his wrist, drawing blood.

He brought it to Lilan's lips, "Lila, you have to drink this. It'll help ease the pain."

Lilan let out a low, shuddering breath as the venom ran through her body, making it almost impossible to move. Thane gently placed his wrist against her lips, helping her, "Please, Lilan, don't die on me.

Please." After a few heartbeats, he pulled his wrist away, staunching the flow. Her cheeks were flushed, but she was alive. Thane was relieved. Now he had to find a place to stay and keep her safe. He let his senses spread out.

There, up a little ways on the hill. Life. Quickly, he picked Lilan up and started for that direction. Thane could smell a sort of pine smell in the air. Suddenly, a drop landed, followed by another. He was still in pain, but the lycan venom hadn't kicked in yet in his system. He cast out his senses toward the young girl, checking on her. Thankfully, she was to become a vampire, nothing more, nothing less. Finally, he cast his senses within himself. The lycan venom was spreading through him, heading for his heart. He had to hurry to the area thriving with life, otherwise, the enemy would drag him back.

The rain started to come down harder now, leaving Thane chilled to the bone. There was light from a mansion up ahead. Quickly, he ran toward the mansion, slipping through the mud. Lilan fell from his arms, hitting the mud softly, unmoving. Thane got up a bit from the ground, reaching out and crawling up the stairs. He knocked quickly on the door, before falling back down onto the stairs.

The door opened, revealing a male with black hair, blue tips flashing in the light from the hallway. His eyes widened, "What's this?"

Thane raised his gaze up to look at the male. "Please," He rasped, "Help the girl. The enemy...held her prisoner. Help her...help us." His body grew numb as the lycan venom took over, causing him to lose consciousness, "Help..." He fell, landing hard onto the stairs, and remembering no more.

Chapter 14

Thane bowed his head, "After that, they took us in. Story told, good night."

Asuka held up a hand, "Wait, you mentioned someone named Axis? How evil was he? Was he like Xanatos?"

Thane shook his head, "No. He was more into scaring others with stories and rumors, other than actually using his power, like Xanatos." He sighed, "He was resurrected a few times, and like always, I was there to stop him." He looked away, "With Xanatos, I've gotten a few scrapes, cuts, broken bones, that kinda thing."

She narrowed her eyes, "But, what happened to Lilan? You were injected with lycan venom, and then you bit her. Wouldn't see turn into a hybrid, instead of a vampire?"

Thane cast a hard look at her, "I wondered that myself. According to several notes kept by Lilth, lycan venom is slower than vampire venom, making their victims suffer in agony."

Asuka nodded, "That vampire that killed Alena and captured you, she sounded an awful lot like Ivory."

Thane nodded, "Back then, I didn't get a name, never got a chance to. And it's been so long that I completely forgot about her. Guess our little confrontation she and I had before must have jogged my memory."

"Huh? What confrontation?" She asked, puzzled.

"Oh yeah," Thane shook his head, "Forgot you were passed out after she bit your hand." He sighed, "After she first attacked you, she and I fought." A smile graced his lips, "Guess she was a little intimidated by some of my moves and power, because she didn't stay long. What a wuss and a waste of a good fight."

Kursed softly cleared his throat, "Hate to break up this cozy little session, but dawn for all vamps is just about here. I'm afraid I'll have to retire for the rest of the night." He got up and strode over to the door.

Asuka shook her head, "So, it's true then. All vampires burn in sunlight."

Kursed looked back at her and smiled, "No, we can go out in daylight just fine, we just don't like it, too bright. Also, the sleep heals any wounds we acquire." He waved, "Night."

Thane sighed, yawning, "And it's time for this old pup to take a small nap."

Asuka shook her head, "What?"

He laughed, soft and rich tones that made her shiver slightly, "Forget already, princess? I'm a hybrid. Sure, part of me is a vampire, but the wolf in me still needs rest every once in awhile. Also, it cancels out most of the weaknesses on both sides."

She nodded, "I've been wondering about that. Could you…possibly tell me a bit about hybrids, since they're still a new species, in a way."

He slowly nodded, "I'm guessing you're curious about this life, aren't you?"

"Is it obvious?" Asuka sighed, "Better know all I can if I'm to be sired."

His eyes went from emotionless to showing a bit of sympathy, "You don't want what happened to us, happening to you, right?"

She didn't say anything, letting him continue.

"Oh boy, where to start with this one?" Thane pinched the bridge of his nose, "Well, being a hybrid doesn't make us invincible. We can get hurt, and possibly killed." He growled, "Bleeding out, as I told you Alena did, can weaken, and possibly kill us. Everything is magnified when us, including passion. We can eat normal food, but can't have too much of it, otherwise we can get really sick."

Thane sighed, "But we have to watch the lycan side. Because part of me is now an animal, I tend to lose myself, when there's either a fight, or I catch the smell of blood. The lycan side, though, requires a lot of rest, so I can stay alert and ready to fight." I can go out in daylight just fine."

He yawned again, "But I am getting tires, and tomorrow night is the hunt. You have to be ready."

Asuka shuddered, "Don't remind me."

He gently laughed, "Just get some sleep, I'll see you in the evening." He walked over to the door, and walked out, quietly shutting it behind him. Asuka yawned once, before laying down against the pillows, and blacking out, dreaming dreams of shadows and red eyes.

Thane stood outside her door, face in one hand, breathing hard. Quickly, several memories flooded back into his mind, from his earlier days with the rebels.

Thane, snap outta it!

Hold him there!

No good! He's too strong!

Lynx, ready the tranquilizer!

On it!

Fire!

His eyes snapped open, breath ragged and shallow. He sank to his knees, trying to dispel the memories. Ever since he had been around this girl, this mortal, memories had come flooding back, making him sick to his stomach everytime he saw them. He didn't want to remember what he did before. Thane took in a soft breath, slowly letting it out. It was time to rest.

***

Lilan ran straight into Asuka's room and leapt onto her bed, "Get up, get up, get up!" She ripped the sheets back, exposing Asuka's warm, toasty flesh.

She let out a piercing cry, curling into a small ball. "Not now, mommy," She moaned, puling the blankets back up, "Five more minutes."

Lilan looked up at Thane, "Well, your turn!"

Thane raised an eyebrow, an evil plan coming to mind, "Alright, fine." He knelt beside the bed, raised a single hand up, and slowly dragged his fingers over a very sensitive spot on the back of her neck.

Asuka sat up quickly, skin crawling as she screeched, "Who did that?"

Thane raised a hand up, chuckling, "Guilty."

She looked over at him, eyes narrowed, "You enjoy teasing me, don't you?"

He rolled his eyes, "And you enjoy yelling at me, don't you?"

"I wouldn't have to yell at you if you just stopped with the teasing," She growled.

Thane thought for a moment, then, "Nope. More fun to watch you squirm." He came forward, "Now, where else are you ticklish?" His eyes took on a dangerous glint as a wide smile spread across his lips. He scooted closer to her, raising his hands up and started to bring them down toward her sides.

Lilan loudly cleared her throat, "When you two are done acting like children, the others are ready for the hunt." She turned and left.

Thane sighed, getting off of Asuka, "She's right. We'd better get going." He started to get up.

Asuka bit her lip, wondering what to do next. Without thinking, she reached out and poked Thane's sides, hoping for a response. He didn't move at first, body stiff. Slowly, he turned around. "Asuka," He whispered, "Trying to see if I'm ticklish, are we?"

She quickly shook her head, "N-no, I'm not. Honest."

He slid over onto the bed, slowly pinning her down. He chuckled, bending down to whisper in her ear, "Maybe I'll give you a chance later tonight, all alone, where I'll make you squeal."

Asuka's face turned red as her eyes widened, "You'll never make me squeal."

He laughed softly in her ear, making her shiver in delicious delight, "Is that a challenge?"

She narrowed her eyes, "Take it as you will, Thane."

Thane held her a bit tighter, "Wrong answer, Asusu."

For some reason, she didn't mind it when Thane used her childhood nickname. In fact, it sounded right when he whispered it softly, as if she belonged to him. He chuckled, "No answer then? Maybe I should make you squeal again. It was kinda cute." He bent toward her throat, fangs bared, "Maybe you'll squeal when I sire you."

She closed her eyes, breathing hard, "Thane, you win. Stop now."

He chuckled, "No, I don't think so. Not yet." His breath was hot against her throat, making her breathe a bit quickly, skin tingling.

She gasped, chest rising up and down, "Thane…stop. You win." He moved closer, gripping the back of her neck, making her suck in a breath.

There was a knock on the doorway, alerting the two of them. Kursed stood there, leaning against the doorway, a sly smirk upon his lips, "Catch you two at a bad time?"

Thane quickly got off of Asuka, the smile gone, "No, Kursed. I was just about to head out."

Asuka let her body drop back onto the bed, breathing hard. Thane had once again, teased her, and she had fallen for it. Seemed to get a major kick out of it. She shook her head, getting up, and following after Thane.

"Kursed, wait, please."

All three of them turned around to see Meagen standing there, face a little red, "Kursed, I kinda need to take a bit of a blood sample from you, to see if Ivory still has some control over you." She took his hand and pulled him along, "It'll only take a second."

Kursed's eyes widened, "Wait, you plan on using a needle, right?"

She nodded, "Only way."

He smiled at her, then waved, "Good bye!" He started to turn to run.

Meagen cast Thane a look, "Thane, if you please?"

He nodded, as if in understanding, "Yeah, I know." He reached out and gripped Kursed's shoulders, pulling him back, "The more you struggle, the more it'll hurt."

Meagen came closer to Kursed, seriousness painted all over her face. She pulled out a syringe, "Please, Kursed, just let me get this sample."

"What brought this about all of a sudden?" Kursed asked.

She blushed heavily, "I...kinda overheard you guys sharing stories, and I heard the part where we met, and since Ivory's still alive..."

"You figured you'd take a small sample of my blood, to see if I'm still being controlled," He sighed.

She nodded, sticking the needle into his arm. He hissed, the arm stinging a bit, "And since Ivory's infiltrated out home more than once, I thought, somehow, you two were still connected." She pulled out the needle, "There, all done!"

Kursed sighed in relief, "Good, that's over with."

She waved, "Have a nice hunt, guys!"

Asuka threw her a curious look, "You're not going?"

Meagen shook her head, "Nope, never do. I prefer to stay inside." She winked, "Have fun!"

Thane shook his head, "Let's go." He turned on his heel, and started for the door, Kursed and Asuka following after him.

Once outside, a flying object hit Asuka in the face. She pulled off the object to see a shirt in her hands. She rolled her eyes, "Alright, who threw this?"

Cyrus raised his hand up, a wolfish grin on his face, "Sorry, Asuka, that was my fault." Cyro started to remove his pants.

Kursed quickly pulled Asuka over to him, shielding her eyes with his hand, "Have you two no shame? No decency?"

Cyrus thought for a moment, then, "Nope, not one shred of decency." Cyrus went to remove his pants.

Cyro rolled his eyes, "Come on, Kursed. We're lycans. We don't wanna rip our clothes when we change. If Asuka can't handle it, oh well."

Asuka pulled out from Kursed's grip, shaking her head. She looked over at Cyrus and smirked, whistling, "I think the full moon is out tonight."

Cyrus looked around eagerly, "Where? Where is it?"

Cyro sighed, "It was a joke, brother."

Cyrus's smile grew, "Hey, Asuka, you're about to see something cool! Ready?" She nodded, eyes wide.

Cyrus smile stayed as he groaned, doubling over, as if in pain. His breathing became ragged as popping sounds shot through the air. He growled as his face started to shift, growing a muzzle, teeth lengthening into canines. His fingers bent to look like claws as his nails lengthened as well. Fur started to sprout everywhere, black as the night. Silver, lightning-like symbols circled around all four legs. Around his ears was a dull grey color. He let out a loud, final howl as his tail grew out, soft and bushy. Cyro stood next to him, almost an exact duplicate of his brother, save for the silver fur.

Asuka shook her head, releasing the breath she was holding inside, "Cyrus, Cyro..."

Kursed chuckled, "Speechless?" He took her around the waist, smirking, "Come on, Asusu, lemme show you how a true vampire hunts." He took off, holding her tightly as he leapt forward. She closed her eyes, refusing to watch the scenery fly past, lest she want to get sick. Suddenly, he stopped, sniffing slightly.

She tried to find her voice, speaking softly, "K-Kursed?"

Kursed smiled, "Food's near. Give me a sec." He took a cautious step forward, feet apart, waiting to spring.

There was a rustling sound near the bushes as a young man stumbled through, eyes wide while he held a knife tightly in his hands. He brandished it at Kursed, smelling of cheap drink, "Wha' do ya want, punk? I swear, I'll rip out your bleedin' throat if you come closer!"

Kursed smiled, "I'd like to see you try." Without warning, he pounced onto the man, squeezing his wrist and ripping deep into his throat, emitting a small growl as the man went limp.

Asuka squealed slightly, hand covering her mouth, eyes wide. Kursed didn't budge for a minute, until he finally brought his head up, blood staining his lips. He gestured for Asuka to step closer, "Come on, you need to taste human blood before you can be sired." Asuka shook her head, fear immobilizing her body. Kursed growled, "Asuka, now!" She shook her head again, turning around, and running deep into the forest.

Kursed growled, "Great, just great." He turned back to the body, and continued feeding.

Asuka kept running, not caring where she would turn up. After some time, she decided to stop and catch her breath. She sat down against a tree, and sighed, slowly closing her eyes. Something brushed against her arm, making her twitch. She brushed the thing aside. The thing came back, all prickly and hairy. Slowly, she moved her head over to see what it was. A rather large, hairy tarantula was on the tree, raising a leg up as it inched closer. Her eyes widened as she shrieked, quickly scooting away from that tree, breathing hard.

A strong hand came down on her shoulder, startling her. She looked up to see Thane, concern in his eyes, "You okay? I heard you scream."

She raised a shaky hand up and pointed toward the tarantula, "Spi-spi-spider...big spider."

Thane sighed, putting his head in his hand, "You're telling me, you screamed, over a little spider?" He stifled a chuckle, "You're a wuss!"

Asuka growled, "It's not funny, Thane!"

Thane walked over to the tree, "It's just a baby spider." He held out his hand, letting the tarantula walk into his palm. Thane stood there for a few minutes, softly stroking the spider as it sat calmly in his hand, "Aw, look, it can't hurt a fly, much less a human."

Asuka remained tense, "Let...it...go, Thane."

Thane shrugged, "Whatever." He paced his hand against the tree, releasing the tarantula, "Happy?"

She nodded, "Yes, now that you set that creepy crawly free." There was a slithering sound in the brush near her feet. Asuka tensed up again, seeing something long and slim slither by her feet. Her eyes widened, "Sn-sn-snake..." Her words trailed off, seeing the snake raise its head up, forked tongue flicking out as it held her gaze in place.

Thane sighed, "Don't tell me you're afraid of snakes, too." She nodded quickly, not saying a word. Thane bent down and picked up the small snake, letting it coil around in his fingertips, "Asuka, why do you hate snakes?"

She narrowed her eyes, "Let's just say I had some bad experiences at the academy."

Thane never took his gaze off the snake, as he listened intently, "Go on."

She blushed a bit, looking at the ground, "Well, with the snake, some older girls decided to play a prank on me, and put a small, nonpoisonous snake in my bed. It crawled up my pant leg and slithered up my body. I awoke to see it poking its head out from under my shirt. I'm grateful it didn't bite."

He nodded, "And the spider?"

She didn't look at him, "The same girls held me down one day, and brought out a teachers' prized tarantula, and decided to let it walk all over my face. Thankfully, a teacher walked in, before it could get a chance to bite." She shuddered, "Haven't like them since."

Thane shook his head, "Arrogant, idiotic, little freaks." He let the snake go onto the grass, "Come on, we need to hunt in order for you to be sired." He held out a hand to her, waiting.

She bit her lip, before taking it, "Hope you're not like Kursed."

Thane chuckled, "Did the little vamp scare you when he attacked someone?"

She nodded, "Wasn't exactly subtle about it."

He looked back at her, "Don't remember Lilth saying you had to only hunt humans. How does deer sound?"

She made a face, "Worse."

He seemed amused, "Well, if we can't find a human, than a deer will have to do." He sniffed the air, "You're lucky. A human's near."

Asuka came closer, "Why do humans come out here?"

He shrugged, "Place used to be a make out spot for young teens. Heck, it still is. More adults come here now, though." He grinned, "And a human has just stepped right into out path."

A young teen stepped out from the trees, eyes a bit hazy. He cast a lethargic look over at Thane, stumbling as he walked, "Oh, there you are. Wondering where you were, man."

Asuka looked over toward Thane, puzzlement in her eyes. Thane smirked, "He's high, teens like to get high out in these woods." He placed a finger on his lips, silencing her. He carefully walked over to the teen, eyes never leaving the teens' own. Slowly, a smile came to the teen, allowing Thane to relax.

Asuka slowly came up behind Thane, eyes wide, "What did you do to him?"

"Little hypnotizing trick," He replied, "He thinks that I'm an old friend that he's seeing after so long. We should be able to take what we need, and then send him on his way."

She nodded, "Y-you first."

Thane sighed, "Always." He quickly slipped up to the teen and held him still, slicing a nail swiftly into his neck. Licking his lips, he pressed them to the wound, relief flooding inside him, coating his mouth like his favorite drink. Asuka tried her best to ignore the soft slurping sounds until Thane pulled away, holding out his free hand to her, "Come here, Asuka. Come and face your initiation."

She nodded, shaking out of fear. Thane gently touched her cheek, "Just close your eyes. That way, you don't have to watch."

She smiled a small smile, "Thanks, Thane." She bent down toward the small wound in the boys' neck, stomach clenching out of hunger as she slowly licked her lips, mind clouding over. Closing her eyes, she quickly pressed her lips against the wound, taking a small swallow. Her eyes shot open as the blood flowed smoothly into her hungry mouth.

She tightly gripped the young teen, pulling him closer as something stirred within her, a beast of some sort, waiting to be unleashed. Her tongue flicked out over the cut, greedily catching any drop that came her way. When something tried to pull her away, she held on even tighter, growling as she bit down a bit on the teens' neck, trying to get more blood.

"Asuka. Asuka, you need to let go now. Come on, Asuka."

Strong hands came down upon her shoulders, gently pulling her away, "Let go, please."

Asuka brought her head back, eyes wide, breathing hard and ragged. She looked over to see Thane gripping her shoulders, eyes wide, "You okay?"

She looked back at the teen, blood trickling slowly down his pale throat. Her eyes widened a bit more, reaching up to her mouth, "I...I drank...blood..."

Thane narrowed his eyes, "You did well, Asuka, don't be afraid. It was a natural reflex. And, since I didn't bite him, he won't die from the venom. He'll wake up, probably swearing off drugs." He made a face, "His blood made me want to gag, lacked a bit in taste."

She laughed, "Tasted alright to me."

He smiled, "I take it you're ready to be sired?"

She nodded, not saying a word. Thane held out his hand to her, "Come on, let's go back."

Asuka quickly took it, eyes narrowed. Thane helped her onto his back, making sure she was comfortable. He smiled, "Hang on, princess. And try not to watch the scenery as we head back, unless you wanna get sick." Without waiting for an answer, he sped off, blending in with the night. Asuka shrieked, squeezing her eyes shut as the wind hit her face.

"Thane!" She called out, "How much father?"

He chuckled, "Open your eyes, little Asusu."

She quickly opened them to see the mansion, along with Kursed and Lilan. Kursed smiled, "Have a nice hunt?"

Asuka shakily got off of Thane, breathing hard, "Yeah, sure."

Kursed shook his head, "Missed a good meal. The man was a criminal, and decided to hide in the woods. Too bad for him, he crossed paths with me."

Thane winked, "She did a good job for her first hunt." He pushed her forward, "And the night's still young. What do you say to siring you tonight?"

Asuka's face turned red, "Still haven't forgotten your promise from earlier, Thane."

His hands gently came down upon her shoulders, soft chuckling in her ear that made her shiver in delicious delight, "What promise, the promise about making you squeal again, of making me squeal? I forgot all about it."

She rolled her eyes, "Bull." She walked over to the door, opening it to see Lilth standing there. Lilth nodded only once, to get her point across.

Asuka was ready to be sired, and Thane had already promised to do so.

Chapter 15

Ivory cried out, eyes wide as a fiery pain lashed through her body, making it spasm. Xanatos growled, "Again, Aurana, whip her again. Ivory needs to learn obedience, after all."

Aurana grinned with amusement, eyes glowing, "With pleasure, Master." She brought up the whip, laced with silver, and brought it down upon her bare back, creating another large gash running diagonally down her back, close to her neck.

Ivory glanced up at Xanatos, eyes wide, "Master, please, mercy! I beg of you!"

Xanatos came closer to Ivory, gripping her chin tightly in his hand, "Mercy? You want *mercy*?" He slapped her across her face, palm stinging a bit, "You should have killed everyone there and brought Asuka back. You failed on that part, Ivory."

She looked up at him, panting, "They…knew how to fight. Little mutt…is stronger…than before."

Xanatos let her go, "You should have fought back." He nodded once. Aurana smiled, bringing the whip down again, cackling as Ivory screamed, writing in agony.

Ivory growled, blood dripping from her lower lip, thanks to a fang piercing it, "Master, I tried. Thane fought back and protected her!"

Xanatos held up a hand, motioning to Aurana to stop for a moment, "Did you say Thane?"

Ivory nodded quickly, "Yeah, Thane. He was there, all right. Still has those awful grey eyes that seem to search your soul, to cast judgment on you." She shivered a bit.

Xanatos growled, "I thought that old mutt was dead by now."

Ivory quickly shook her head, "He lives, even now!"

Xanatos swore under his breath, releasing her, "So, if he's still around, things may get complicated." He paced away from her, growling, "God, he's strong, for his breed."

Ivory nodded quickly, "Yes, he is."

Xanatos locked eyes with her, Tell me, does Kursed still run around with Thane?"

Ivory shrugged, wincing a bit, "I think so."

He smiled, "Good. Bring him back to our side, maybe he could…convince Thane to join as well. Or maybe bring Asuka to us."

Ivory smirked, "I think I can arrange that."

His smile grew, "Good. Don't fail me again." He nodded at Aurana, who brought the whip up a final time, then brought it down, ripping deep into Ivory's flesh, making her scream.

***

Asuka sighed, resting against the glass of her window, icy cool against her warm hand. The hunt was hours ago, and that had left her drained and exhausted. Now was the next step, becoming a dark creature, and leaving her old life behind.

Her skin tingled as she imagined how Thane's bite would feel. Her eyes slowly closed as vivid images started to form in her mind. She shivered as she felt a soft piercing sensation on her throat. There was gentle nibbling added as he drank from her, making her breathe a bit faster. A quiet moan escaped her lips, as invisible hands caressed her body.

Soft chuckling broke her out of her fantasy, making her turn around. Thane stood in the doorway, smiling a sly smile, "Oh, don't mind me, I'm just enjoying your little fantasy."

Asuka growled, "I didn't ask you to intrude upon my fantasies, Thane."

He rolled his eyes, "Part vampire, remember, which means I can pick up on your thoughts."

She looked away, "I forgot about that."

He laughed softly, coming close, "Well, are you prepared, little Asusu?"

Asuka smiled nervously, "Y-yeah, I am."

Thane smiled, "Good." He gently touched her shoulder.

She pulled away, "Wait, how do I know you're not going to seduce me the way you seduced countless others?"

Thane laughed, "Do I have to spell it out for you?" His lips gently descended upon hers, making her suck in a breath. His hands slowly wrapped around her, holding her close as he nibbled a bit on her bottom lip, seeking entrance. Her mouth parted, eyes closing slowly as she ran her hands up his chest. He pulled back, eyes mere slits as he smiled, "Is that proof enough?"

She nodded quickly, "Come here." She pulled him back, softly kissing him. Gaining a response, he wrapped an arm around her waist, pulling her close. Her breathing quickened, eyes rolling back as her eyelids slowly closed again. His tongue snaked into her mouth, making her moan softly, running her fingers through his hair.

She pulled away, breathing hard, "Okay, so you were telling the truth."

Thane took her by the hand and led her over to her bed, "I told you." She sat next to him, body aching for his touch once more. He obliged, hands gently caressing her body, making her whimper in pleasure.

She leaned her head back, moaning softly, "Do it, Thane, please." Her chest rose and fell as her body began to heat with passion, "Do it."

He pulled away, moving down to her arched throat. God, what was this girls' power, and why was she able to do this to him? He didn't care about the answers. All he cared about was her blood as body. He growled, kissing tender spots here and there. Whenever he hit a correct spot, she would moan and whimper. Deciding to tease a bit, he let his tongue flick out, licking the more sensitive spots near her collarbone and shoulders. She groaned, silently begging for Thane to just bite her already.

Thane pulled back, feeling something inside him yearning to take over, wanting to rip into her throat, spill her blood. But his sanity squashed those urges, as he held her, waiting for the shivers to subside from her. He smiled, "Was I that good?"

Asuka couldn't speak, body yearning to feel his touch again. After a few seconds, she managed a single word, "Wow."

He chuckled, "Then let's continue." He started to pull her back, eager to taste her blood. Asuka winced a bit, her midsection throbbing again.

She smiled gently, "I'm sorry, Thane."

He shook his head, "It's alright." He brought his wrist up, quickly slicing into it, "Here, drink it. It'll help."

She eyed the wrist, feeling her stomach grow as if in response. Slowly, her tongue slid over her lips, "Y-you sure?"

Thane laughed, "Don't worry. You'd have to receive my bite to start the change. Taking in my blood can heal wounds and give strength." He gestured the wrist toward her, "Go on, it'll help you."

She let out a soft sigh, gripped the wrist in her small hands, and pressed her lips to the wound, swallowing. Thane's eyes slowly closed, as he tipped his head back, growling softly. Relief flooded through her, as the pain in her sides slowly vanished. She growled, pulling Thane closer, and laying a kiss upon his lips, pushing him down against the sheets.

Thane laughed, "Trying to be the dominant one, are we, little Asusu?"

She chuckled softly, "If you'll let me."

Without a word, he pulled her back down, hearing a savage roar scream in his head as each and every kiss made his skin tingle. His tongue flicked her lip, seeking entry, which she gave to him, body close to near agony with wanting him.

He pulled away, breathless, "Close your eyes, little Asusu." He softly kissed her throat, "Close your eyes, and I'll give you what you want."

Asuka slowly felt her eyes close as she tipped her head back, "Do it, Thane. Take all you need."

He felt his fangs lengthen as he growled softly. Quickly, without thinking, he used a lengthened claw, and made a small, shallow slash into her neck, blood beginning to ooze a bit down. Licking his lips, he bent down toward the wound, and began to drink, eyes slowly closing in ecstasy.

Thane could literally see inside this girls' mind. Her hope, her bravery, and kindness all mingled together in his mind, while the taste was exquisite on his tongue. It had a sweet taste to it, with a small hint of a vanilla taste, mixed with lavender. He could feel her emotions jumbled together like a hailstorm beating against his head. Slowly, a memory came to mind, one from her past.

A beautiful woman came into a living room, breathing hard, "Asuka, you have to hide, now!"

A small, redheaded child looked up from the floor, hazel green eyes wide, "Mommy, what is it?"

The woman picked up her daughter, burgundy hair concealing a bit of her face, "Just trust me, alright? We have to get you hidden, now!"

She carried the small child up a set of stairs near her, trying to keep her breathing even. Quickly, with a shaking hand, she opened the door on her left, pushing the child inside, "Hide in the closet, Asuka, and don't come out until you're sure it's safe."

She nodded, "Be careful, mommy." She dashed quickly inside, pulling open the closet and running inside, closing the door behind her. Breathing shallow, she peeked through the slats on the door, listening with strained ears.

Her mother could be heard outside the door, muffed words being exchanged. There was a loud sound, like a smack or a punch, she wasn't sure which. "Mommy," She whispered, breathing a bit quieter.

Her mother was thrown inside the room, a person following behind her, "Did I take you away from all your toys, Hunter? Too bad." The person raised a hand up, smacking her hard across the face.

Her mother growled, "What do you want with me, hag?"

The woman growled in response to her, raven black hair hanging down her back, "My master has given the order to exterminate all

*Hunters, including you. And he has ordered for me to take your child."
She raised a dagger up, "Guess what I get to do first?"*

*Her mother lashed out with her foot, trying to connect with her face.
The woman laughed, as she grabbed her ankle, holding her in place,
"Is that your big attack? A kick?" Her grin widened, "You're fighting
against a vampire, mortal." She brought the leg up a bit higher,
twisting the ankle to the breaking point.*

*Her mother screamed falling to the floor like a wounded animal,
"You'll never find my daughter, wrench! She's long gone!"*

*The woman laughed, "She's hiding in this room, lowlife. And I'll
find her once I'm finished with you." She brought the dagger up, and
thrust it through her mothers' chest.*

*There was a loud scream as the woman twisted the blade. Cackling
madly, she repeatedly stabbed the childs' mother several times, before
getting up, licking the dagger clean. Looking back down at the corpse,
she kicked it once, before turning away.*

*She giggled, "Little Asusu, where are you?" She started for the
closet, hand outstretched.*

*There was a loud bang on the door, followed by multiple footsteps,
"Hurry! Fan out and find her! If you spot the vampire, kill her. Save
any survivors."*

*The vampire looked over toward the door, cursing loudly. She cast
a final look toward the closet, before sprinting toward the window,
glass shattering around her.*

*The child relaxed, grateful the vampire was gone. Hot, salty tears
rose in her eyes, falling down her cheeks, "Mommy." Slowly, she
curled up into a small ball, and began to cry.*

*The closet door was opened, light streaming inside, illuminating
her small frame. She sniffled, looking up to see a young teen with stony
grey eyes, hand outstretched, "You can come on out, it's alright."*

The child bit her lips, as she gently took his hand.

Thane broke the contact as his eyes remained closed, trying to shake
off that memory. So they had met before when Ivory had murdered
Asuka's mother in cold blood. No wonder he acted the way he did
around her. He shook his head, looking down at Asuka.

Her skin was a bit pale, as her eyes remained closed. He gently touched her cheeks, her face. Great, he took a bit too much. Thane sighed, bringing out a small pocketknife and making a small mark on his neck. Lifting Asuka up with the other hand, he gently brought her up, "Come on, Asuka, you need to drink. Please." No response, "Asuka, please." Thane guided her to the spot, holding her head there, "Please." He closed his eyes.

Something flicked out, greedily catching any drops of blood that came into her hungry mouth. Thane felt relieved as his arms slowly came around her, holding her close as she drank, strength returning.

Thane felt his vision start to fade a bit as his head swam. He must have forgotten what it was like to lose blood, instead of gaining it. Gently, he pulled her away, trying not to harm her.

Asuka growled, eyes lustful as her tongue snaked out, catching any stray drops that clung to her lips. Her breathing came out fast and hard as she sat there, unmoving. She reached out to Thane, eyes wide, "Thane…"

He caught her as she started to fall, body singing with new life. Quietly, he stroked her hair, resting his head on top of hers, "I'm here."

She sighed, "Well, did it work?"

Thane bit his lip, closing his eyes, refusing to tell her the truth, "Yes, it did."

She snuggled closer into his, "Never even felt the bite."

He nodded, "I know." Without another word, he fell asleep, tightly holding onto Asuka.

***

Meagen slammed both hands down upon the table, growling softly. On the monitor in front of her, was a small blood count, showing small signs of black clinging to the red blood cells. She bit here lip, drawing blood, "Great, just great."

Soft footsteps came up behind her, placing a hand on her shoulder, "Something wrong, Meagen?"

She jumped, eyes wide as she looked over at Kursed, "I'm fine, Kursed, just fine."

He chuckled in her ear, "Don't look fine to me." Kursed put a hand under her chin, "In fact, you look troubled. What's wrong?"

Meagen shook her head, "Just running tests, is all."

Kursed looked at the screen, eyes narrowed, "Doesn't look good for me, right?"

She wiped a few tears away, "No, it doesn't."

"Hey," Kursed rested his head on top of hers, "There's no reason to cry about it."

Meagen shook her head, placing her hand down onto the table, "Ouch!" She pulled her hand back, cursing. On the table was a small scalpel, used during one of the tests. She pulled her hand up to see how bad she was cut. A small, thin trickle of blood started oozing a bit down, deep ruby red in the dim light.

She growled, "See what you did?" She looked away.

Kursed brought her face back to look at him, "What did I do?" He brought up the bleeding finger and softly kissed it, making her suck in a small breath. He pulled her close, "Did I hit a nerve?"

Meagen growled, "Kursed, please, don't do this."

He smiled, "Don't do what?" Gently, he kissed the finger, slowly putting it into his mouth, sucking on the wound.

She tipped her head back, shuddering a bit, "Kursed, we shouldn't do this."

He pulled away from her finger, smiling a bit, "Why not?"

Meagen shook her head, "Because...you like Asuka, that's why."

Kursed chuckled, "As a sister, Meagen. She's like a younger sister to me." His arm snaked around her waist, "You, on the other hand, have been there for me. Plus, you were the first person I met when I changed sides." His eyes softened, "Give me one good reason why we shouldn't do this."

Meagen shook her head again, "Because...I'm not who you think I am. I'm..."

He came closer, "You're what, Meagen? In case you haven't notices, we're all monsters, in a way. You may think you are some evil monster, but I see a beautiful, intelligent young lass who I wouldn't mind loving."

She quietly wiped tears away, "Kursed, I..."

He didn't give her a chance to speak. His lips descended upon hers, making her suck in another breath. Meagen rolled her eyes back, body shivering as she ached for his hands to touch her. Kursed did so, hands running down her back and halting at her waist, holding her there.

Meagen moaned, letting her arms slip around his neck as his tongue snaked into her mouth, fang piercing her lip. Pulling away for a bit, he began to trail kisses down to her throat, fangs brushing against her skin. She took in a shuddering breath, "Kursed, please..."

Kursed growled in response, letting his tongue flick over her jugular, making her cry out softly. Quickly, without giving her a choice, he plunged his fangs into her neck, tasting blood.

Meagen tipped her head back, her breath coming out in rasps. She let her arms go limp, as Kursed slowly sipped from her. After awhile, he pulled away, gasping for breath. Her blood was different than Asuka's blood, more rich in flavor. It also had a small, sweet kick to it that left him wanting more. He looked down at her, as Meagen was trying to shake off the lethargic feeling. She pulled away, "I have to go."

Kursed's eyes widened, "Why?"

"I've got to get this to Lilth," She sighed, "Look, it's not you, right now, because that was amazing." She sniffled, "I...I just need some time to think about this, alright?"

He nodded, "Yeah, that's fine with me." He ran a hand through his hair, "Just...hurry back, Meagen, please."

She cast a final look at him, before taking off out into the hall.

Kursed sighed, "Way to go, tough guy. You came on too strong, and chased her away. Real smooth."

"Talking to yourself, Kursed?"

Kursed spun around to see Ivory standing behind him, crimson eyes filled with amusement, "What's the matter, no words for an old friend?"

Kursed took a step back, eyes wide, "Ivory, w-what are you doing here?"

Ivory smirked, "I was in the neighborhood, and thought I'd drop by." She raised a hand up, backhanding him across the face.

His body was flung back, hitting the table, "Get out of here, Ivy! The others will kill you if they find you here!"

She laughed, "Let them try, little fire puppet!" She gripped his shirt collar and threw him against the table, away from the computer monitor. "Now listen, and listen good," She hissed, fangs bared, "Seeing as how I'm still kicking, I guess I'm still your master."

Kursed growled, "You're not my master, Ivory!"

She smiled, bringing her wrist up, "We'll see about that." Quickly, she bit deep into her flesh, drawing blood.

His nose twitched, taking in the scent of blood. His hand shook slightly as he reached out toward it, licking his lips, "Ivory…"

Ivory smiled, "You want it, Kursed?" She pulled it away, "Then join back up with me."

Kursed shook his head, "No way, Ivory."

She growled, slowly licking away the blood. She leapt forward, straddling him, and preventing any means of escape, "I know how to make you join." Biting her lip, she bent down and kissed him, forcing his lips open with her tongue. She jumped as a fang pierced her tongue, drawing more blood. Her blood filled his mouth, making him snake an arm around her waist and pulling her close, eager for more.

Her lips curved into a dangerous smile as her hands slid up his chest, nails memorizing almost every inch. He groaned, trying to get to her bottom lip, which continued to bleed freely.

Ivory pulled away, breathing hard, "So, how about it, Kursed?"

Kursed sighed, growling, "Ivory…I can't."

She pretended to pout, lower lip sticking out, "Why not, Kursed?"

He looked away, "Because…I don't like you like that."

She frowned, "So, it's that Meagen girl, isn't it?" She smiled, claws unsheathing, "Maybe I should give her a makeover, see if you like her then." She started to leave.

Kursed gripped her wrist, pulling her back, "No, wait!"

Ivory paused, slowly turning around, "Yes?"

He sighed, "You win. J-just don't hurt Meagen, please."

She narrowed her eyes, "And what's she to you?"

He lifted his gaze up to her, biting his lip, "She's…everything to me. She makes me smile when I'm upset. Whenever she's happy, I'm happy, too." He shook his head, "She was the first person I met at that club."

She helped him up, wrapping both arms around his waist, "You'll have to forget about her now, Kursed. You'll have to forget about everyone. It's time to come home."

Hid eyes fell slowly closed as he sighed, "Yes, my master."

***

Asuka stirred next to Thane, sore and groggy. Slowly, she opened her eyes, seeing an arm slung around her waist, almost in a protective way. She smiled a small smile, stretching. Her neck tingled a bit, remembering Thane's touch, his kiss.

His teeth.

She shook her head, eyes narrowed as she tried to remember all that happened. He had made love to her, of that, she was certain. Sire, he made her feel like she was flying. But she couldn't remember his bite, the bite that would change her. She growled softly, holding her head in her hands.

A soft, gentle touch came down on her shoulder, making her jump slightly, "What's wrong, Asusu?"

She looked around, seeing Thane's concerned face staring back at her, "I'm fine, Thane."

Thane smiled, "Good." He reached out for her, pulling her back, "Come here, you."

Asuka squealed in delight, but was cut off by his lips descending down upon hers, while his hands danced along her body. She moaned softly, feeling his lips trail down to her exposed throat. Tightly, she gripped his shirt, body shaking, "Thane, please…"

Something gripped a bit too tightly on her hair, pulling her roughly back. Asuka let out a small cry, "Thane, that hurts! Please, stop!"

Thane didn't listen as he pulled her head back, growling. Without another word, he sank his fangs deep into her throat, claws digging into her flesh.

The scream in his head made Thane shoot up, breathing hard, eyes wide. Quickly he looked over at Asuka to see her sleeping peacefully. He sighed, running a hand through his hair

A small scent touched his senses, growing in intensity. His eyes widened even more as he recognized the smell. Thane quickly reached out for Asuka, shaking her, "Get up! Get up!"

She stirred, slowly opening her eyes, "Thane, what are you doing?"

He growled, "Do you smell that?"

Asuka paused, sniffing a bit. Her eyes widened slowly, "Fire!"

Chapter 16

Thane reached out, gripping her hand, "Come on, let's go!"

Asuka jumped up, scrambling to get onto her feet, "Where is it, Thane?"

He shook his head, "I don't know!" His gaze flicked around the room, finally pausing at a small fire burning near the bookshelf in the corner. Quickly, it spread over to the bed, traveling around the hanging curtains surrounding it.

Thane growled, "I think I know who started this, but I'm not sure if I'm right!"

Asuka let out a small cry as the flames brushed lightly against her ankles, "Thane! We need to get to the others!"

"Right!" He took her hand and pulled her along, heading over to the door.

The fire spread over to the door, engulfing it. A beam fell from the top, landing over the door knob, and blocking a means of escape. Asuka let out a small cry. "We're trapped!" She cried out. Sh coughed a bit, the smoke entering her lungs.

Thane looked around for any quick ways of escape, "There! The window!"

Asuka gripped his arm, gulping, "Are you sure?" The curtains around the windows flared up, flamed burning cheerfully.

Thane nodded, "Yeah, positive!" He gripped her tightly around her waist, "Whatever you do, don't let go, and don't look down!" Asuka coughed, nodding.

Thane nodded, "Hold on!" Asuka bowed her head, feeling his grip tightened as Thane began to run toward the window. There was a loud, splintering crash as glass flew everywhere, cutting a bit into their skin. Suddenly, Asuka felt their bodies plummet into the ground, her stomach entering her throat as the cold air stung their faces. Asuka let out a small cry as she gripped his shirt, the ground looming closer.

There was a loud grunt of pain and surprise as they landed, sprawling onto the ground. Asuka let out a small groan as she looked over at Thane, "Thane, hey, you okay?"

Thane stirred, coughing a bit, "Y-yeah, I'm good. You?"

She nodded, "Yeah, I'm fine."

He leaned back onto the ground, groaning. Her eyes widened, "Thane, what's wrong?"

He coughed again, "Remove your knee, please."

Asuka's eyes narrowed in puzzlement, "What?"

Thane groaned, "Your knee is kinda in the wrong place. Can you remove it?"

Asuka looked down to where her knee was, to see it between Thane's legs. Her face turned bright red as she quickly scooted away. "I'm...I'm sorry, Thane," She whispered.

He chuckled, sitting up slowly, "It's okay, Asusu, wasn't complaining. In fact, if our lives weren't in danger right now, I would have enjoyed it." He paused, eyes narrowed, "Asusu, get down!" Thane leapt forward, grabbing her tightly and pulling her down as something whooshed overhead.

Thane growled as something sharp pierced his right shoulder, the arrowhead tip sticking out through the skin. He howled, gripping the arrow as blood oozed out onto his hand.

Asuka jumped up, eyes wide, "Thane, lemme help you!"

He growled, pushing her hands away, "No, you can't! If you remove the arrow, I'll bleed out!"

Soft clapping made them both jump, slowly looking behind them. Ivory stood leaning against a tree. "Look at the two of you," She crooned, voice low and deadly, "It's so sweet, I'm getting a few cavities." She shook her head, chuckling, "Kursed, come on out and say hello. You did start that fire, after all."

Out from the shadows stepped Kursed, a small smile upon his lips, "Hello, little ones."

Thane growled softly, "What are you doing, Kursed?"

Kursed laughed, "Obeying my master, is all." He narrowed his eyes, growling, "I suppose I could ask you the same, Thane."

Asuka's eyes narrowed in confusion, "What does he mean, Thane?"

Kursed smiled, "You mean you couldn't figure it out? Why didn't you feel his bite? Supposedly, he has a harder bite than other hybrids. Where was the pain? The venom was supposed to render you paralyzed for awhile, while the change began taking place in your body." He smile grew wider, "Answer me, little Asusu."

Asuka looked over at Thane, hesitant to even speak, "Thane…is that true? Is that all true?"

Thane refused to look at her, eyes locked with Kursed's own, "I had my reasons."

Kursed growled, "Tell her the truth, Thane. She deserves to know."

Thane sighed, looking over at Asuka, "It's true, all of it."

She refused to look at Thane, "You mean…you didn't sire me?" Asuka rounded on him, "Why? Why didn't you do it?"

"Because I cared about you!" He exclaimed, "And…I didn't want to see you hurt."

Kursed chuckled, gently gripping her shoulders, "He couldn't sire you, because of his own weak feelings." He nuzzled the space between her shoulder and throat, gently licking a sensitive spot. Asuka let out a soft cry, disgusted at herself as her body shivered in delicious delight. Kursed softly nibbled on her ear. "If Thane couldn't sire you, I can," He whispered.

Her lip trembled, voice shaky, "And if I refuse to let you?"

His grip tightened on her as his fangs brushed against her bare skin, "Then I'll bite you and drain your blood until you're a lifeless corpse. Finally, I'll leave you for the lycans."

Thane made a move toward them, hand outstretched. Kursed pulled back on Asuka's hair, pulling her head slowly back, fangs bared, "Come any closer, and I'll bite her here. You want that on your conscious?"

Thane growled, trying to think of a quick plan, "Don't suppose I do."

Asuka let out a small cry, eyes wide, "Thane, don't even think about it!"

It was too late. Blending in with the shadows, he vanished on the spot, aiming for Kursed's head. He whipped out a small blade from within his boot, reappearing, as he brought it down for a killing blow.

A sharp pain lashed into his side, kicking him away. Thane landed a few meters away, breathing hard as he tried to get up from the ground. He looked up to see Ivory, her crimson eyes narrowed in amusement.

Asuka growled, "Thane, don't!"

Thane looked over at her, "Shut up!"

Asuka bit her lip, "Don't, please! If you have to, think of a plan to save me later, then do it! Don't try to save me now!"

His body shook in anger, "What about you?"

Asuka let out another loud cry as Kursed pulled her hair again. Her breathing was shallow, "I'll be fine, trust me!"

Kursed smiled, "What do we have here?" He moved some of her hair aside to reveal a small cut, still clotting over, trying to heal. He slowly licked his lips, "Thane still left his mark on you. Well, don't mind if I do." He raised a nail up, slowly reopening the wound. Blood began to drip down her neck, warm and slow against her heated skin. Teasingly, Kursed licked a hot trail over the cut, the blood flowing into his hungry mouth as he drank, holding her tightly.

Ivory smiled, "You try to attack either of us, Asuka will get killed." Her eyes narrowed dangerously, "Feel free to attack and take your chances, but either way, she'll die."

Kursed lifted his head up, the bloodlust in his eyes, "Man, Thane, you should have shared, she's delicious."

Thane lashed out at them, but Ivory cut him off, "So, I take it you want her to die, huh?"

Asuka let out a gasp, "Thane, please, don't worry about me for now!" She sniffled, tears falling down her cheeks as she watched him struggle with getting up, "Just promise me…you'll come save me…when you've thought of a plan, alright?" She met his eyes as she silently begged for him to stop the useless fighting, "Please, Thane."

Thane gave her a final look, before bowing his head, "Alright, fine. You win." He looked up at Asuka, "Just…just keep faith that I will come save you."

Asuka nodded, "I know you will."

Kursed growled, pulling Asuka up by her hair, "Get up, filthy whore!"

She whimpered, but didn't say a word. Gripping Asuka tightly, he and Ivory took off, blending in with the night.

Thane growled, feeling anger rise within him. Bringing up a fist, he brought it down, crying out into the night, howling a single, painful word.

"No!"

***

Ivory threw Asuka inside a dark room, Kursed following behind her, "Get in there, worthless tramp!"

Asuka whimpered in fear as the large door locked, trapping her. She gulped, trying to find her voice. "W-where am I?" She whispered.

Gentle, consoling hands came down upon her arms, wrapping her in a loving embrace, "Easy now, Asuka. Relax, you have nothing to fear."

Her body froze at the sound of that voice, making her blood run cold, "Xanatos."

Xanatos chuckled, bringing his lips against her ear, gently nibbling on it, "You sound so frightened, Asuka. I assure you, there's nothing to be afraid of."

Asuka turned her head to look at him, "Why do you want me so bad?"

Xanatos smiled, "Because a rose of fair beauty should be allowed to bloom freely, in front of others, then to be locked away, hidden from view." He nuzzled the crook of her neck, chuckling, "Besides, your beauty far surpasses most. A trait I love in women." He tenderly kissed the spot there, making her shiver in revulsion.

He chuckled, "Ivory, show her to her room. My new plaything needs a place to stay. Remember, she only gets the best."

Ivory growled, "Whatever." She gripped Asuka's arm and began dragging Asuka away, "Let's go, whelp."

Asuka snarled, "I can walk on my own."

Ivory bared her fangs, I suggest you keep silent, wrench." She opened a door on her left, shoving Asuka roughly inside, "Clothes are in the wardrobe. Breakfast is a sunup, dinner at sundown. You don't eat, oh well." She stalked forward, shutting the door behind her, "You will wear a chain most of the time, unless Xanatos wants to feed." She smiled, "Give me a second to find it." She turned toward the wardrobe in the corner, bustling around in the drawers.

Asuka took her chance to launch a kick at Ivory's midsection, connecting with a few ribs. Ivory doubled over, hissing as she tried to grab Asuka, "Little tramp! Get back here!"

Asuka ignored her, running for the door and flinging it open. Kursed stood on the other side, smiling a wicked smile, "Leaving so soon?" He started forward, baring his fangs, amused to see Asuka trembling in fear. "Stay awhile," He said, "We were just getting ready to have some fun." His eyes glinted a bit, coming closer to Asuka, "Besides, Xanatos may let us have a sip later on."

Asuka gulped, "A-a sip of what?"

Kursed chuckled, "Your tender blood."

Ivory nodded, "It's so rare to find those of pure blood now. Almost everyone is getting raped pr committing other crimes or sins. You don't quite realize just how delicious you smell. So…appetizing." She bared her fangs, growling.

Asuka turned to run, but Kursed gripped her arms, holding her back, claws digging deep into her flesh as they left small marks. He bent toward her throat, chuckling, "Of course, we won't take until Xanatos gives us permission."

Ivory growled, "I'm not waiting. Give her here." She brought a nail up, slicing into her shoulder. Asuka cried out, feeling blood trickle down Ivory smiled, coming closer.

Kursed snarled, "No! Xanatos has not given the order!" He smiled, "Besides, there will be plenty of time later, after Xanatos has gotten a taste." He gripped her tightly, "Find that chain, and let's put it on her!"

Ivory nodded, "Right!" She went back to the open drawer, pulling out a large shackle attached to a chain, "Found it!"

Kursed tightly gripped Asuka, as she continued to struggle, claws continuing to dig deeper into her flesh. He growled, "Wait." Narrowing his eyes, he deliberately ran his tongue slowly over the fresh cut Ivory had made, cleaning up the blood, "Now you can put it on."

Ivory smiled, quickly placing the shackle and snapping it into place, "There, let her go."

Kursed let her go, the ground cold against her skin. Kursed reached out, gripping her chain tightly in his hands and yanking her forward. "Get up, little Asusu," He chuckled, "Get up and play!"

Asuka growled, eyes narrowed, "You'll find I won't be broken so easily."

Ivory smiled, "We'll see about that." She aimed a kick toward her ribs, knocking her down, "Get dressed, wrench. Xanatos will want you to join him in the Great Hall soon." She turned to leave, Kursed following behind her."We will return shortly," Ivory whispered as they walked away.

***

Thane growled, slamming his fist into the table, leaving a mark, "I should have done something!"

Meagen placed a consoling hand on his shoulder, eyes wide, "You shouldn't be so hard on yourself."

He growled, "But she was trapped! I should have done everything I could!"

Cyrus narrowed his eyes, "Yeah, and you would have lost Asuka if you did."

Thane felt rage rise within him, begging to be released in a loud scream, "And I didn't want that!" He looked at them, "But, if you had only seen her eyes, or felt her fear, you would have tried as well."

Meagen nodded, "It must have been hard."

Thane growled, "She was so…afraid."

Soft footsteps came up behind him, "While we were putting out that fire from earlier, you confronted them, didn't you?"

Thane nodded, staring off into space, "But…I couldn't…"

Lilth smiled, "I know." Her eyes narrowed, "But you promised Asuka that you would save her, yes?" Thane nodded once, "Well, then for now, why not switch sides?"

Thane glared at her, "You're mental!"

Lilth sighed, "Like it or not, it may be a good way to keep Asuka safe." Her eyes softened, "You can watch over her, keep her safe from harm. I don't like this either, but it may be our best shot. Maybe you can sneak her out of there or something. For now, keep her safe."

Thane gave her a hard look, before nodding once.

***

Xanatos sighed, feeling tired. He would get to see Asuka tonight, before he rested during the dawn. He slowly closed his eyes, imagining all the things he would do with her. Both Ivory and Kursed had reported that her blood was divine, very rare tasting. He let out a soft moan as he imagined the taste of her blood, coating his mouth.

Soft footsteps sounded next to him, making him jump and turn around, "Ah, Thane, how nice to see you."

Thane growled, "Spare me the politeness. It makes you look fake."

Xanatos growled, "Killjoy. What do you want?"

Thane bowed, "I've come to humbly offer my services to you, Xanatos."

He curled his lip, "And why should I believe you?"

Thane growled, eyes flashing dangerously, "I'll prove my loyalty in any way I can."

Xanatos let a smile curve his lips, "Any way, huh?" He beckoned for Thane to follow, "Come." He led Thane up a flight of stairs, finally opening a door on his left, "After you." Thane stepped quietly inside.

Inside was a large bed, draped with luxurious curtains. Near the window was a tall wardrobe, door slightly ajar. And on the bed was a slim girl, fiery red hair a mess, silver chain hanging off the bed.

Thane bit his lip to keep from crying out her name. Quickly, he thanked whomever was looking out for her, as Xanatos slowly walked in, a long whip in hand. He chuckled, "Well, here's your test, Thane."

Thane had to restrain himself as he kept his voice steady, "What is this, Xanatos?"

Xanatos held out the whip to Thane, who took it. He strode quickly over to Asuka, quickly yanking on her chain, "Get up, little Asusu. You have company." He yanked the chain hard, pulling her out of the bed, "Now!"

"Don't harm her!" Thane exclaimed.

Xanatos growled, "She caused some trouble earlier. Thane. Your test is…to punish her."

Asuka stared, horrified at the whip, "No, please."

Thane glared at Xanatos, "Why whip her, Xanatos?"

Xanatos smirked, "Because I was told you both have something…special between you two." He rested his chin in his hand, "What better to break her spirit, then to have the one she cares about break her."

Thane growled, bringing up the whip. Asuka's eyes widened, "Thane, don't, please!"

Xanatos came up behind him, laughing softly, "Do it, Thane. Whip her. Trust me." His voice dropped to a low hiss, "Trust me."

Asuka shivered, "Thane…please…"

Xanatos's eyes glowed brightly as he smiled, "Do it."

Thane slowly raised the whip up, then swung it down, lashing against Asuka's skin. Asuka cried out, falling to her side. She looked up at Thane, eyes pleading as she whispered his name, "Thane…"

Xanatos growled, "Again, Thane."

Slowly, the whip came up once more, as Thane quickly brought it down, creating a gash on her lower back. Asuka screamed in agony as her body shook. Again, the whip came down on her, as she writhed in pain. She looked up at Thane, lip trembling as she tried to speak, but trailed off at the sight of his emotionless expression, his eyes filled with icy coldness. For the final time, Thane raised the whip up, and swung it down upon her back.

Xanatos held up a hand, "That's enough, Thane."

Thane lowered the whip, face blank, "Are we done here?"

Xanatos nodded, "Quite Leave the ship here, and bring her out with you, Thane."

Thane nodded, "And your trust with me?"

Xanatos smiled, "It has been proven, Thane. Welcome to the family." He walked out the door.

Thane gripped the chain tightly, "Get up, Asuka. It's time to go."

Asuka refused to look at him, shaking her head, "You'll have to force me."

Thane growled, kneeling beside her, "Asuka, I don't want to hurt you, though."

She looked up at him, eyes blazing, "Then what was the whipping for? To show your dominance? News flash, Thane, you'll have to try harder than that."

He rolled his eyes in irritation. Sighing, he gripped the chain and pulled her forward, walking for the door.

Asuka struggled, trying to pull the chain away from her. Annoyed, Thane yanked hard on the chain, making her fall forward onto her face. He snarled, "Asuka, let's go!"

She glared up at him, picking herself up off the floor. Voice dripping with venom, she spat two words to him, livid, "Screw you."

Thane shook his head, before leading her out the door.

Chapter 17

Xanatos smiled as the large door opened, a low creak echoed around the large chamber. "Finally," He called out, "Our new guest has arrived, and he brought our new toy with them." The crowd roared in pleasure and delight as Thane stepped forward, dragging the struggling Asuka behind him.

Thane yanked her forward, knocking her off of her feet, "I brought her, my master."

Asuka could barely believe the words coming from Thane. He had changed, become cold. His eyes had even lost their warmth, leaving her soul cold and terrified. She was now in the viper's nest, and one wrong move could cost her, be it her sanity, or her life.

Xanatos growled, "Asuka, step forward."

She shook her head, eyes wide, "Never!"

Xanatos snarled, "Thane, bring her to me."

An iron grip came down upon Asuka as she was dragged forward, being pulled over toward Xanatos. Xanatos grinned, "Welcome, little Asusu. Sorry about punishing you earlier. It hurt me to watch."

Asuka growled, "If you were sorry, you'd let me go."

Xanatos shook his head, "Sorry, little one. I can't." He pulled her closer to him, hot, coppery breath brushed against her face, "You're mine now. And I have no desire to let you go."

Asuka curled her lip, spitting at him. Xanatos snarled, wiping away her spit. Fangs bared, be brought a clawed hand up, and smacked her across the face, leaving four, tiny marks, "Don't you dare do that again, slut!"

Asuka growled at him, "I do what I please."

His hand shot out, grabbing the spot under her chin and lifting her up, meeting his eyes, "You'll do what I say if you value your life." Smiling, he raised a nail up, letting her see it, "Now, hold still. This will only hurt if you struggle."

Asuka tried to back away, tried to flee, but Thane held her close, unmoving. Xanatos brought the claw down, slicing the top of her exposed chest, thanks to the skimpy top she wore. Growling, he bent his head down toward the spot, and slowly licked a path over the fresh cut, making her shudder in revulsion. Finally, he pressed his lips against the wound, and began to drink.

Asuka writhed against him, eyes wide, "Lemme go, please!"

Xanatos lifted his head up, blood staining his lips, "Not a chance, little Asusu."

Asuka growled, "Let me go, or I swear, you'll regret it!"

Everyone in the room cackled and jeered, eyes flashing dangerously. Xanatos chuckled, "You think I'm afraid of your little threats or friends? He smiled, "I'm not. In fact, I look forward to facing your friends."

Asuka growled, eyes filled with malice, breathing hard, "Just you wait, Xanatos, just you wait."

His grin grew, "Well, while we wait, how about you dance for us?"

She shook her head, "No way!"

His smile vanished as he backhanded her across her face, cheek stinging. "You will dance for us, filthy tramp!" He spat, flexing his hand as he reached for a whip beside his throne, "Dance, or be punished, your choice."

Asuka cast him a livid look, before taking a step back onto the middle of the floor. Slowly, she raised a leg up, spinning around, the bells on her shoes jangling cheerfully. Thanks to the lightweight pants and the skimpy top, she was able to breathe freely. Her red hair fanned out like fire, hazel eyes filled with unshed tears.

Xanatos smiled, relaxing, "Thane, answer me something."

Thane nodded, "Yes?"

Xanatos chuckled, "You've probably made love with her once or twice, right?"

Thane gave him a questionable look, "Yeah, so?"

Xanatos smiled, "I plan to have some fun with her soon. Maybe I'll claim her as my mate, and bring her over." His eyes closed as he began to enjoy his little fantasy, "Just imagine it, a dark little angel. One who will be obedient and carry out my every whim. And her lusts will be insatiable, like my own."

Thane made a small little noise as he looked away, "Yeah, right."

Xanatos grunted in response, "You say something, Thane?"

Thane shook his head, "Asuka has too much free will. She'd never obey you."

Xanatos grinned, "Maybe if I get someone else to do the deed, she'd be obedient."

Thane curled his lip, "What are you suggesting?"

Xanatos chuckled, "I give you a bit of my blood, Thane. You go to sire her for me. Bring her over, and my blood runs through her veins."

Thane shook his head, "No way. If she gets sired by me, she'd be mine, and mine alone."

Xanatos scoffed, "Please, she's a lowlife mortal. What joy could she possibly bring you?"

A growl escaped Thane as he looked away, "I like my possessions."

Xanatos nodded, "Of course, of course." He slowly licked his lips, "Then I guess the deed is mine, and mine alone."

Thane focused on Asuka as she danced, the dim light casting shadows on her skin. His eyes narrowed as he took in her slim frame, the way her hips moved and swayed from side to side. He could just imagine running his hands down her body, nipping and sampling her blood while she moaned in pleasure. He could practically feel the lust rise within him as his breathing sped up a bit.

Xanatos growled, "Asuka, that is enough."

Asuka fell to the floor, breathless as she looked up at him, chest rising up and down, "Yes, Xanatos."

Xanatos growled, bringing up the whip, "Asuka, do I have to remind you on what to call me?"

She curled her lip, "I won't call you that."

Xanatos raised the whip up, bringing it down against her arm, "Now, what do you call me, little one?"

She growled, eyes narrowed, "Never."

The whip slammed down hard against her arm again, making her cry out, "What do you call me?"

Asuka glared at him, breathing hard, "M-master."

Xanatos lowered the whip, waving his hand, "Dismissed. You are to be escorted back to your room, and await further orders."

Asuka had already pulled herself up off the floor, and was bowing at Xanatos, "Yes, master."

Xanatos nodded, "Thane, take her away."

Thane reached out and gripped her chain, pulling her along, "Let's go."

Asuka reluctantly followed behind him, looking down at the ground.

Xanatos rested his chin on his hand, smirking, "Ivory, I want you to do me a favor."

Ivory materialized from the shadows, a small smile upon her ruby lips, "Yes, master?"

Xanatos looked up at her, "Slip Thane a bit of your blood. There's some in the black bottle in our wine cellar." His eyes narrowed, "I want him to be an obedient little mutt who sings pretty like a wolf." He chuckled softly, eyes glowing.

***

Asuka growled, trying to pull away, "Let me go! I can walk on my own!"

Thane growled, "Will you just shut up for a minute? I swear, you're like a broken record, going on and on about nothing! It's driving me insane!"

"I wouldn't act like a broken record if you'd just let me go!" She cried out, trying to pull the chain, earning a hard yank in the process, "Now, let me go!"

Thane opened her door and pushed her inside, following behind her and closing the door, "Are you insane? Are you trying to blow my cover?"

Asuka scoffed, "What cover? You're just like Xanatos and everyone else in that room! If you were here to save me, you would have done it by now!"

"And risk everyone coming down upon us?" He asked, growling. Letting out a breath, he slowly shook his head, "Sorry, but being around these kind of people has kinda made me wary of others."

Asuka turned away, "Did you have to whip me in front of Xanatos?" Her lip trembled a bit, as anger and sadness filled her eyes.

"Would you rather I had died in front of you?" Thane asked, placing gentle hands on her shoulders, "Asuka, I've been around guys like Xanatos before. They're ruthless." He bowed his head, "I've seen good people get slaughtered by this guy. I don't need to see anymore die."

Asuka looked up at him, sniffling, "Have you...been under his control before?"

He nodded, voice hoarse, "Yeah. I came back to them after awhile, during an assignment. I was supposed to go in, find our missing comrades, and help them escape. All of us were called into his execution room, where each person was ripped apart and fed to the lycans." He shook his head, "Lilth had told me to be a good little boy, and don't blow my cover. That night, I ran, barely escaping with my life."

Her eyes widened in shock, "Oh, Thane. I had no idea." She turned back around and pressed herself against him, letting tears fall, "I don't wanna lose you, Thane. You're all I have while I'm here."

He nodded, "I know. And rest assured, I will try to protect you." His eyes slowly closed, "I promise."

Asuka pulled out of his grasp, wiping tears away, "But Thane, how are you going to protect me? I'm cold, tired, hungry, and aching. No one else wants to help me, but you. And what will Xanatos say when he starts to notice you helping me?"

Thane growled, "I won't give him a chance to notice." He gently kissed her forehead, "Listen, I gotta go for now. But I promise, I will be back.'

Asuka started up at him, eyes wide, "Please, hurry back."

Thane nodded once, "I will." He walked over to the door and excused himself.

In entered a young woman as Thane left, carrying a tray, "The master wishes for you to eat something." She lifted up the silver lid, exposing a large chicken breast smothered in barbeque sauce, "So, eat up." She placed it on the table next to the bed.

Asuka gave it a dark look, "I'm not hungry."

The woman laughed, "It's not poisoned. I assure you that. Now, eat."

Asuka looked away, "I'm not hungry."

The woman sat up, growling, "Fine, starve for all I care. You're an ungrateful little brat anyways." She turned to leave.

Asuka gave the food a final thought, before going over and getting ready to eat.

***

Exhaustion finally getting to him, Thane started down the corridor, hoping to find a spare room.

"Thane, do you have a moment?"

Thane paused, body tensing as if waiting for an attack, "Who's there?"

Out from the shadows stepped Ivory, a small smile upon her lips, "Easy, mutt, I'm not here to fight."

He narrowed his eyes, "What do you want then?"

Ivory held out her hand, "To show you to your room. Master told me to put you up in one of our best rooms." She bowed her head, "If you will please follow me, I'll show you the way." Ivory turned around, and began to lead the way.

Thane growled, muttering to himself, "Stay calm, be a good little mutt. You're no good to Asuka dead."

Ivory stopped by a door with a polished handle, chuckling, "Talking to yourself? Good, makes me feel like I'm the sane one around here." She opened the door, gesturing inside, "Go on. I assure you, there's nothing in there that will kill you." He ignored her comment, and stepped inside.

The room was round, with a balcony window. A chandelier hung from the ceiling, casting a golden glow upon everything. The bed was huge, lined with silk, crimson sheets. Across from them was a medium-sized table with a large black bottle and two wine glasses. Thane growled, "Expecting to share a drink with me?"

She shook her head, "It's not wine, Thane. I will say it is quite lovely." She unscrewed the top and poured out two equal amounts, the liquid dark and clinging to the glass.

Thane curled his lip, lightly sniffing the air, "It's blood, aged, but still fresh."

She nodded, "Mongrel has a good sniffer, I must say." She grinned, taking a sip, "Afraid to drink it, are you?"

Thane was about to snap at her, when Lilth's warning echoed in his mind, *Remember, Thane, keep your head down, and nose clean. You may have a better shot to save Asuka.*

He smiled, "I'm not afraid of a little drink." He gripped the glass tightly in his hand, taking a long swallow.

His mind felt a bit hazy at first, as his body swayed for a moment, making him feel like he was beginning to float. He stumbled forward for a second, before everything finally stopped, his vision returning.

Ivory smiled, "Too strong?"

Thane shook his head, "No, just felt a bit funny for a minute there, is all."

She grinned, "Funny, huh?" She placed her glass down, red staining the sides of her glass, "Thane, tell me what you're feeling right now?"

He growled, "Wish you'd set Asuka free." He clasped a hand to his mouth in shock, eyes wide.

Ivory smiled, pressing herself up against him, "Say something else, anything else! How do you feel about Asuka?"

Thane shook his head as he forced his hand away, "She's beautiful, kind, caring, and an angel!" He backed away from Ivory, panicking, "Whose blood was that?"

She chuckled, "Mine. And you tasted it, like a good little mutt."

He brought a fist back, and slammed it into her gut, breaking a few ribs in the process, "Why?"

Ivory glared up at him, eyes livid, "My master ordered it. He said he wanted you to be obedient, for once."

Thane shook his head, "I won't let you control me."

Ivory growled, spitting blood out of her mouth, "It's too late. My blood is already inside you. You have no choice." Her eyes narrowed, "On your knees, mongrel."

Thane felt his body shake as he tried to resist, tried to fight back against her control, but he fell to his knees, gasping for breath. His eyes were wide as he looked up at her, "S-stop it!"

She gripped his hair, pulling his head back, claws against his throat, "I can't stop it, love. Like I said, it's already too late." She bent down and gently kissed his lips, releasing his head as her hands gripped his shoulders, holding him down.

Thane struggled, kept his lips firmly closed. She growled, tried to nip at his bottom lip to get a reaction. He tried to bring his hands up to shove her away, but she held on, refusing to let go. Ivory straddled him, as she pulled away, eyes narrowed. Growling, she gripped both of his arms, and forced him back onto the ground. Without a word, she bent down and kissed him again, tongue forcing his lips open. Thane let out a small growl as he bit down on her tongue, making her pull away, crying out in surprise.

A shadowy tendril shot up, wrapping around Ivory. Thane met her eyes, his own blazing, "Just who do you think you are?"

Ivory smiled a sadistic smile, "Your master's sire." She giggled, "And you got a taste of my blood tonight, twice. I guess that would make me your master now." She growled, "Now, release me, Thane."

He growled, shaking his aching head, "Never!"

Her voice dropped to a low hiss as her eyes began to glow, "Release me."

Thane's body tensed as the shadows dropped from around them. Ivory smiled, "Good boy." She chuckled as she came closer, pressing her lips against his own, hard enough to bruise. She let her hands explore every inch of his body as she bit his lip, drawing blood. He tried to push her away, but she held his arms down, growling.

His mind went blank as it started to shut down, giving in. *So this is how I lose everything,* He thought to himself, *At the hands of a blood thirsty tramp.*

Come on! What kind of talk is that?

Thane tried to focus on the voice, tried to just think, *W-who are you?*

Oh geez, you're screwin' with me! You can't sit here and tell me who I am? Figure it out! I've been with you for so long, buddy. Don't you think it's time to let your true power show? The speaker let out a loud chuckle, *Now, take care of this slut, and go get your girl, Thane!*

Thane growled, *Who are you, though?*

For crying out loud! Who do you think?

Thane tensed in shock, recognizing the voice. It was his own, back from when he was ruthless, cold as ice. Well, whoever the voice was, it was right. Anger began to rise within him, causing shadows to rise up, and separating the two of them. Ivory launched back, the back of her head slamming hard into the opposite wall. Slowly, her body fell to the ground, landing facedown and unmoving.

Thane took in a shuddering breath as he tried to calm down. God, that felt…*good.* It felt wonderful. He tried to stifle a chuckle, lest Ivory would pull herself up and attack. But she didn't. Her body lay still, taking in shuddering breaths.

Good! Nice job! Now, go and claim your woman! Asuka's in danger! She needs you!

Wait a minute, Thane thought, *How do you know?*

We shared blood with her, duh! Now get it together, and save her! Meagen and Cyrus are on their way.

And how do know that? He growled.

If you had opened your mind a bit more, they would have sent you a message, idiot! God, I wise you were your old self again! You never would have let yourself get caught like this!

Thane had to resist a snarl, *Shut up!*

Then go to Asuka, for Christ's sake! Get her outside and to safety!

Whatever, Thane growled, heading for the door.

***

Asuka sat up in the bed, the sound of the doorknob turning. Her eyes widened as she smiled, "Thane, welcome back!" Her smile vanished as Xanatos walked inside, a slim, long pole in his hand.

Xanatos grinned nastily, "Sorry, but no. I'm your companion for tonight."

She warily eyed the pole, body tensing, "What are you doing with that?"

"Oh, this?" Xanatos chuckled, an evil glint in his eyes, "It's not much, just a small branding iron I use to mark all my little playthings." He brought it up, letting Asuka see the small circle with a star in the middle of it, "Now, hold still. I need to mark you."

Asuka let out a small cry, trying to get around him. Xanatos reached out and smacked her across her face, knocking her down to the ground. Straddling her, he held both of her hands down with one hand, and brought the iron closer. "I don't think so," He hissed. He pressed a small switch on the pole, turning it on, "Come on, I need to do this. I don't need another man claiming you before I do." He started to bring the branding tip down upon her exposed waist, grinning an evil grin.

The door burst open behind them, anger vibrating off of the figure in unseen waves. Thane stood there, eyes filled with unbridled anger. Xanatos turned around, eyes wide, "Thane?"

Thane raised an arm up, slamming hard into the side of his head. His eyes rolled back into his head as he crumpled to the ground, losing consciousness.

Thane turned toward Asuka, breathing hard, "You okay?"

Asuka nodded quickly, "Y-yeah."

Thane held out his hand to her, "Come on! We gotta get you outta here!"

She nodded, "Of course, but where do we go?"

Thane growled, "Meagen and Cyrus are on their way here as we speak. They'll take you back."

Asuka shook her head, "No, I won't leave you behind!"

"You have no choice!" He snarled, "Would you rather be trapped here, until you died?" Asuka looked away, refusing to answer.

He sighed, "Can we go already? The sooner you're safe, the sooner I can relax."

Asuka nodded, biting her lip, "Alright, fine." She took his hand, tightly grasping it. Thane held her trembling body close as he felt himself begin to meld with the shadows, the cold biting his flesh.

Asuka let out a small cry, the fear rising within her again. Soothingly, Thane stroked her hair, murmuring soft words of comfort.

Once outside, they materialized near the shade of a pine tree, both gasping for breath. Thane looked down at Asuka, eyes wide with love, "You okay?"

Asuka nodded, licking her lips, "Yeah, I am now."

"Asuka!"

"Thank God you're okay!"

Both Meagen and Cyrus came up to them, both wide-eyed and out of breath. Meagen wrapped the exhausted girl in a tight embrace, "We were so worried about you!"

Cyrus nodded, "We thought you were a goner!"

Asuka wiped joyful tears away, "No, thank God, I'm not a goner." She looked over at Thane, "He saved my life."

Cyrus ran a hand through his silver hair, "Yeah, we kinda convinced him to join Xanatos for now. That's how we were able to get to you."

Asuka looked over at Thane, eyes wide, "Come with us, Thane."

Thane shook his head, "No, I can't."

Her lip trembled as his words sank in, "Why?"

He looked away, running a hand through his hair, "If I were to leave now, I may never get another chance to find the Xanatos's weakness." He gently kissed her forehead, "Please, Asuka, let me go."

She growled, "No way."

"Do you think I have a choice?" Thane spat, eyes wide, "Look, if I find a weakness, great. If not, then I'm screwed. Either way, I'm not just

152

gonna sit around and do nothing!" He sighed, looking at her, "Trust me, little Asusu, we will be together." He hugged her tightly, "Come and get me and Kursed when you feel you're ready." His eyes hardened as his eyes met hers.

Asuka relaxed as she bit her lip, "Do it, Thane."

Thane brought his arm up, and swung it toward his head, a loud crack echoing in the air. Asuka let out a small cry, before crumpling to the ground, breathing ragged and shallow.

Thane glared at Meagen and Cyrus, "Get her to safety. Don't let her try a rescues attempt until she's sure she can handle herself."

Meagen looked back at Thane, "What about you?"

He looked back at the old castle, a grimace on his face, "I have to stay here for now. I can't leave this time." He growled, "Now, go and get her out of here."

"How long will she be out?" Cyrus asked.

"An hour, possibly two," Thane said, "Just get her out of here, before anyone finds out she's gone."

They both nodded, getting Asuka up into Meagen's arms. Meagen cast a final look at Thane, "Be careful."

Thane nodded, "You guys be careful as well."

Meagen bit her lip, before taking off with Cyrus, both becoming blurs in the darkness.

Chapter 18

Asuka stirred, waking up in brightly lit room, Cyrus sat next to her bed, his breath held. Asuka groaned, "What's going on?"

Cyrus sighed in relief, "Thank God!" He looked up toward the shadows, "Hey guys, she's awake!"

Asuka slowly sat up, eyes closed as her head continued to pound, "Not so loud, please. How long was I out?"

Cyrus shrugged, "About an hour or so. I dunno. The rest of us were trying to set up a few plans to finish this once and for all."

Quick footsteps entered the room, leaving Cyrus to trail off. Meagen appeared beside the bed, breathing hard, eyes wide, "You're awake!"

Asuka nodded, "Think we've established that already." She rubbed the side of her head, "Man that hurt, though. How hard did Thane hit me?"

Cyrus thought for a minute, then, "A little hard. You were a bit pushy to stay, though."

"Way to put it bluntly, though," Meagen rolled her eyes.

Cyrus nodded, "Thanks!"

Asuka felt her heart freeze as she remembered everything that happened, up to the point where Thane had rescued her, and stayed behind to gather information. "I gotta go," She said.

Meagen pushed her back, shaking her head, "No way! You're not going anywhere, Asuka!"

Asuka glared at Meagen, "They have Kursed, too. Did you know that?"

Meagen looked away, avoiding her gaze, "No, I didn't."

Asuka narrowed her eyes, "Do you plan to leave him there?"

Meagen turned slightly red as a low growl escaped her lips, "No, I don't plan to leave him there! I plan to rescue him...once I think of a plan."

Asuka shook her head, "Look, I gotta go. And you're not going to stop me." She pushed past Meagen and Cyrus, stumbling for the door.

Cyrus reached out to her, pulling her back, "You're not even properly trained. You could get killed just walking through the door."

Asuka growled, "So?" She reached up to her neck, feeling something gone, "The shackle! It's gone!"

Meagen nodded, "We got it off the minute we got you inside."

Asuka smiled, "Thanks." She started for the door again.

Meagen stayed put, biting her lip, "Are you sure you wanna go back there, unprepared?"

Asuka's hand stayed on the doorknob, hesitating, "If I don't go, I may never get another chance." Her eyes hardened, "I have to do this now."

Cyrus gently touched her shoulder, "Asuka, Thane told us to not let you go until you were sure you could handle it."

Asuka wiped angry tears away as she glared at him, "Cy, I have to do this." She looked down at the ground, voice barely a whisper, "Please, let me go."

His eyes widened as Cyrus understood her feelings, "Asuka, we're not going to hold you back, but we can at least prepare you, for in case you get attacked." He took her hand, "Come on, let's get you suited up."

***

Xanatos howled in anger, eyes blazing, "She...escaped?!"

Thane bowed his head, "What can I say? Her friends over-powered me, and took off with her." He shrugged, "Maybe your security needs to be upped a bit."

Xanatos snarled in anger, baring his fangs, "That wrench! She'll pay for this with her life! I swear it!"

Thane chuckled, "Geez, never seen you act like this before. Kinda makes you look childish."

He rounded on Thane, eyes wild, "Shut your trap, filthy mutt!" Xanatos looked over at Ivory, growling, "And where were you when all this happened?"

Ivory swore under her breath, "Incapacitated, thanks to the flea-bitten mutt over there."

Thane smiled, "I may be flea-bitten, but at least I'm not a filthy tramp like you."

Ivory snarled, "Say that again!"

Thane chuckled, "Want more, Ivory? Bring it, anytime, anywhere."

"Enough!" Xanatos growled, eyes narrowed, "Fighting gets us nowhere. We need to think of a plan."

Kursed stepped forward, eyes glinting, "If I may, master."

Xanatos nodded, "Yes?"

Kursed smiled an evil smile, "I have a feeling our little girl will return to us."

Xanatos cocked his head, eyes narrowed in puzzlement, "How so?"

Kursed chuckled, "Thane and I are here. You really think she'll leave us here, while the others try to bring you down?"

Xanatos let out a small chuckle, "Well, Kursed, you're right, of course." He rubbed his hands greedily together, "You and Thane will lay in wait, while the girl makes her way in to see us. No one attacks her…yet." He looked over at Thane, "What do you say?"

Thane smiled, eyes glowing, "I think it may be fun, for all of us." He chuckled as the shadows grew around them, darkening the room.

***

The wind whipped and lashed into her face as Asuka zoomed through the forest, the motorcycle purring under her handling. The motorcycle was Thane's own, as Meagen had told her sheepishly. But she was confident that Thane wouldn't care if Asuka used it to get to them.

Asuka closed her eyes for a few minutes as the wind blew through her fiery hair. Slowly, she opened them, seeing a low branch speeding her way. Asuka cried out, the branch hitting her face as she tumbled off, the bike speeding away into the dark.

Asuka growled, "Good job, Asusu." She sighed, slowly getting up and brushing herself off, twigs sticking in her hair.

She looked around, seeing a dark, looming castle near the stalling bike. She shrugged, "Well, better go in and say hello." She quickly ran up to the dark, heavy door and carefully pulled it open, slipping inside.

It was dark, with rats scurrying around by her feet. Asuka swore softly as one scuttled across her boot, squeaking loud enough to wake the dead. Asuka shook off the creepy feeling she got, and quickly ducked inside an empty room.

The door shut quickly behind her, locking in place. There was soft chuckling behind her, followed by soft footsteps, "Tell me, what are you doing in a place like this?"

Asuka whirled around, eyes wide, to see Kursed behind her, walking slowly, as if taunting her. "Kursed!" She exclaimed, "What do you want?"

Kursed smiled, chuckling softly, "Oh, not much." He rushed forward, pinning her against the wall, "Just a little slut to bring back to my master, Ivory."

Asuka growled, eyes blazing, "You should talk, seeing as your master is one."

His grip on her hair tightened, making her swallow a cry, gritting her teeth. Kursed bent down to her throat, gently taking in her scent. He chuckled, breath hot against her skin, making her shiver, "God, you smell so delicious." His fangs gently touched her neck, not yet biting down, "If Xanatos and Ivory didn't want you, I'd take you for myself."

Asuka let her body relax slowly, taking in slow, even breaths. She tilted her head back, closing her eyes, "Do it, then, Kursed. If you want my blood so badly, then just take it." She waited for an answer.

Kursed laughed, "So, you're willing now, eh?" He pressed his lips against her throat, gently sucking a bit on the skin. She gasped as she felt his fangs about to pierce through the skin. Growling, she brought her knee up, kneeing him in the groin.

Kursed doubled over, gasping for breath as he let her go. Taking a chance, Asuka started for the door.

"Oh no, you don't!" Kursed exclaimed, reaching out and grasping her ankle. Asuka cried out, falling hard onto her side.

Kursed growled, crawling up to her and pinning her down. He bared his fangs, eyes wild, "Trying to get away, huh?" His claws dug into her flesh, making her bleed, "I don't think so!" With one hand, he slid down the front of her body, reaching down to her belt stuffed with small knives and tools. Quickly, he unclasped it and threw it aside.

Asuka had to swallow the curse she wanted to throw at him, to be able to speak freely, "I've got plenty more where that came from, Kursed."

Kursed growled, "I'll find each and every little weapon. He bent down toward her ear, chuckling, "I'll find them, even if I have to strip you down to the last article of clothing."

She tried to wiggle away, "I won't give you that chance, Kursed."

He snarled, gripping her hair and slowly lifting her up, and shoved her roughly against the wall. Kursed bared his fangs, "Thane should have sired you when he had the chance." He grinned, bending down to her exposed throat, "If he didn't have the stomach to sire you, then I guess it's up to me." He opened his mouth and began to bite down, making her shudder in revulsion.

She scrunched up her eyes, breathing hard, "Thane!"

Kursed paused, pulling away. "Thane?" He asked, eyes narrowed, "He's not going to save you." He smirked an evil smirk, "In fact, if he was here right now, why, he'd be helping me."

Asuka tried to pull away, "He wouldn't help a coward like you."

Kursed put on a face of mock shock, "*Coward? Coward* am I?" he brought a hand up, and slipped it under her chin, looking deep into her eyes, "Guess all of us are cowards, at some point in time." He nuzzled the crook of her neck, running a hot path over her jugular with his tongue, "Which means you're probably a coward, as well."

Asuka growled under her breath, slamming her head into his.

Kursed swore loudly as he held his head, swaying a bit. Seizing an opportunity, Asuka tried for the door, the dim lighting casting shadows into the emptiness. He reached out, gripping her arm in an iron grip. Slowly, teasingly, he pulled her back.

Kursed chuckled, "Did you forget, little Asusu? You're fighting against a vampire, child!" He threw her up against the wall again, holding her by the waist, "Are you trying to make me laugh?" His claws dug deep into her flesh, making her cry out.

Asuka glared at him, "Just you wait! Thane will come and save me! He'll kick your scrawny hide any day!"

Kursed brought a hand up, smacking her across the face, leaving claw marks. "You seem so fixated on the fact that Thane is going to save you. Why do you think so?" He asked.

"Because he loves me!" She spat out, eyes wide.

Kursed laughed, "Love? Don't give me that crap!" He came closer to her face, "If he truly loved you, wouldn't he have sired you by now?"

She shook her head. "It was because of love that he didn't do it!" She snapped.

Kursed shook his head, "Again with this love? So pathetic." He chuckled, "It was to gain your trust, little one. Nothing more, nothing less."

Asuka growled, "You don't know him!"

"Then why didn't he bite you?" He snarled, "Why didn't he change you when he had the chance?" She didn't look at him, "Answer me!"

Asuka curled her lip, breathing hard, "Because he actually has a heart, unlike you!"

Kursed laughed, bending down to her ear, "Demons don't have hearts, Asuka."

She looked away, shock registering in her eyes, "That's...that's not true. Thane has to have one. You have to have one."

Kursed slowly released Asuka, chuckling, "Believe me now, Asuka? Thane came to us, seeking to join our ranks." He pulled her into a loving embrace, "Now, Asuka, what I'm going to do is gorge myself on your blood." She tensed slightly, feeling a bit dizzy from his soft, dangerous hiss, "Just relax, little one." He bent toward her throat, about to bite down.

Her lower lip trembled as tears fell silently down her cheeks. "Thane," She whispered, eyes closing tightly.

The door opened, then shut, locking again. There was soft chuckling echoing all around them, "You shouldn't play with your food, Kursed. You might spoil your appetite."

Asuka's eyes shot open as the footsteps came closer, "Thane!"

Kursed growled, pulling away, "About time you got here. Little wrench was giving me trouble." He released her, chuckling, "Go on, Asuka. Go and see Thane. Let him tell you the truth."

She scowled at him before running over to Thane. Thane pulled her into a loving embrace as she shook with fear. "Thane!" She exclaimed, "Kursed told me so many terrible things about you. He said you had actually came here to join Xanatos, not to save me. He said you didn't have a heart." She sniffled, "He said that you used me."

Thane lovingly stroked her hair, eyes full of love, "Do you believe that, little Asusu?" He sighed, "You're telling me, that you believe a friend, over someone who loves you?" he gently kissed her lips, making her shiver a bit in delight.

She pulled away, eyes wide. "Tell me the truth, Thane," She whispered, "Please."

Thane sighed, looking away, "Look, Asuka, Kursed is lying to you. I'd never do that do you."

Kursed growled, "There you go, lying again." He shook his head, "Now, tell her the truth."

Thane snarled, "I am telling her the truth!"

Asuka bit her lip, eyes wide, "Just someone tell me the truth!"

Thane looked over at her, a small smile starting to play on his lips, "Should've believed Kursed. Now you've just screwed yourself." His eyes began to glow with a dangerous tint.

***

Meagen growled, eyes narrowed, "Come on, Cyrus! Hurry up! Asuka could be in trouble!"

Cyrus panted next to her, paws thundering the ground, growling as if to say, "Don't push it!"

She rolled her eyes, "But I feel something's wrong!"

Cyro pulled up onto her other side, letting out a small noise, as if to say, "What?"

Meagen just shook her head, "I don't know! I…I can't explain it! We just need to hurry!"

Lilan ran next to Cyrus, breathless, "Is Asuka going to be okay?"

Cloe nodded nearby, a smile on her lips, "Have faith, Lil! I'm sure Asuka will be fine!"

Sofy nodded, "Yeah, Asuka sounds like a strong girl. She'll probably be fine!"

Lilan growled, "You've never met her."

Sam shook her head, "Just because some of us haven't met her yet, doesn't mean we haven't heard about her at all." She smiled, "Besides, I used to know her mother. Very nice lady."

Meagen growled, "Enough talking! We need to hurry, now!"

They all put on a burst of speed, running to the old, falling down castle.   ***

Asuka shook her head, "No way, that can't be true!" She could feel her heart break as she took a step back from the advancing duo, eyes wide.

Kursed chuckled, "Tried to warn you, Asusu." He started for her left.

Thane nodded, smirking, "But Kursed, the poor girl had to see it to believe it."

Kursed rolled his eyes, "Can't believe she thought you loved her."

Thane shrugged, "It was fun, toying with her emotions, though." His eyes narrowed in amusement, "Poor, pitiful soul, who actually thought her Prince Charming actually cared about her."

Kursed smiled, "Shall we take her together?"

Thane nodded, "Of course." He raised a clawed hand up, "But no one said we couldn't have fun with her first." He snapped his fingers.

A slim, shadowy tendril came up slowly behind Asuka and wrapped quickly around her neck, making her cry out in surprise. She looked frantically from Thane, to Kursed, then back to Thane again. *Their eyes are hollow,* She thought to herself, *They're not Kursed and Thane. Something's controlling them, but what? Or should I say who?*

The tendril jerked back, launching her toward the wall. There was a sickening crack followed by stars in her eyes, blinding her. Asuka coughed, hacking as she gulped down delicious breaths of air. Something hot and sticky slowly oozed down the back of her head, dripping down her neck.

Thane put on a fake pout, eyes narrowed, "Did little Asusu get a little boo-boo?" He cackled, "Good. I want to hear you beg for mercy tonight. I want to hear your screams of pain."

Asuka looked up at Thane, malice in her eyes, "I'm afraid you'll never get that pleasure, Thane."

A boot came up, connecting with her side, making her bite into her lip as a scream threatened to rip from her throat. Several bones snapped under his kick, echoing around them all. Thane smiled, "Still waiting for that beg to slip past those pretty little lips of yours."

Asuka growled, giving him the finger, "That's all I have to say." She tried to get up, but fell back down against the cold, icy floor. She tried to breathe, but even that was tiring.

Kursed growled, "Better show him some respect, little Asusu. Thane is not one to be messed with."

Asuka grinned, "Could have fooled me."

Thane curled his lip as he brought a hand down, pinning her by the throat, "I did fool you, when I made love to you that night."

She brought a hand up, smacking him across the face, "Don't you ever bring up the night to me again!"

Kursed rolled his eyes, "Oh please!" He cast a cold look toward Asuka, "Can we just kill her now! I'm hungry, and we have a perfectly good meal sitting right in front of us!"

"Wait a minute!" Asuka cried out, "Kill me?! I thought Xanatos wanted me alive!"

Thane shook his head slowly, "Not our master. She wants you dead, and out of the picture."

Asuka rolled her eyes, "Ivory, figures she'd get to you, Thane." She tried to pull away, but Thane kept her down.

Thane nodded, "She wants you killed, and your head on a silver platter, so to speak." He quickly pulled her up and shoved her over toward Kursed.

Kursed chuckled, gripping her arms in a tight grip, "Yeah, she feels you're a threat, and out to get what's hers."

Asuka growled, "I don't even like Xanatos! She can have him!"

"You're all he talks about," Thane said, coming closer.

Asuka struggled, "But I don't want him!"

Kursed pulled her arm back and forced Asuka onto her knees. "Still, better to kill you now, then to deal with you later," He crooned.

Thane slowly came closer, licking his lips, "You want first dibs, Kursed?"

Kursed shook his head, chuckling, "She seems to care about you a lot, so you can have first dibs."

Thane nodded, "Fair enough." He placed a strong, firm hand down onto her shoulder, holding Asuka in place. She let out a gasp as Kursed gripped the back of her hair, slowly pulling her head back.

She tensed at the first touch of Thane's lips against her throat, making her shiver in unwanted desire. His fangs scraped her skin, almost piercing through. Asuka bit her lip, eyes tightly shut. *This is it,* She thought, *This is how I'm going to die. By my lover's hand. Or fangs, I should say. Maybe I should tell him how I really feel about him before he drains me.* Her hands curled into fists, *Otherwise, I may not get another chance.*

A bit of a sharp pain made her jump as Thane slowly began to bite down. This was it. Now or never. She opened her eyes as she took in a deep breath, gathering courage.

"I love you!"

Chapter 19

The words echoed around the three of them as Thane paused, tense. He pulled away, eyes wide, "You *what?*"

Asuka took in a breath as silent tears flowed down her face, "I love you, always have, ever since I first met you. I enjoyed the teasing, the love making, everything." She bowed her head, tears spilling down onto the floor, "I was just too afraid, too weak, to tell you. I didn't want you to leave, once you found out the truth."

Thane rolled his eyes, looking away, "And whatever gave you that idea?"

She shrugged, "Maybe it was the way you acted most of the time, with your mood swings and all that. I wasn't sure how you would react."

Thane shook his head, "You really are dense, sometimes."

The grip on her arms loosened a bit as Kursed stood there in shock, barely breathing. *I knew it,* He thought, *I knew it all along. The both really liked each other, but was too afraid to admit it to one another.*

A sharp, stabbing pain sliced through his head, making him cry out. *What are you doing?!* A female's voice screamed in his head, *Attack her, now!*

Kursed's grip tightened on her arm, then loosened, then tightened again. *But...she's my friend,* He thought, *I...can't...*

Do it! The voice screamed, *Now!*

Asuka bowed her head, "I...I didn't want to lose you, though."

Chuckling, Thane knelt beside her, warmth in his eyes, "You'll never lose me, little Asusu." He grunted in pain as something sliced through his head.

Her eyes widened as she held out a hand to him, "Thane!"

You filthy mutt! A female's voice screamed in his head, *What are you waiting for? Kill her, now!*

No way! Another voice shouted, *You have no control over me!*

Liar! The voice screeched in his head, *You got a taste of my blood, and now it runs through your veins.* The voice growled, *Now, kill her!*

Thane held his head in his hands, crying out in a mixture of pain and anger. "Shut up! Shut up! Shut up!" He growled, breathing shallow, "Get out of my head!"

Asuka quickly scrambled to her feet, gently touching his shoulders, "Thane, what's wrong?"

He let out another loud cry, eyes closed as he reached out and swiped for her. Four slashes ran jaggedly down her face, bleeding freely. Thane paused, eyes wide as he took in the sight of her cheek, to his bloody nails, the evidence of his handiwork all over them. He held out a hand to Asuka, trying to speak, but nothing came out.

Asuka took a shaky step back, as she held her cheek, shaking her head, "Thane, what's...what's wrong with you?"

An arm gripped her tightly around her waist, pulling her back. Kursed chuckled, nails digging into her skin. "It's a shame, really," He said softly, "It's a shame that a beautiful woman such as yourself has to die." He chuckled, "Oh well." He brought his face down to the fresh wound on her throat. Asuka squeezed her eyes shut, waiting for the familiar sting, followed by the burning, flowing freely throughout her body.

Thane growled, gripping Asuka by her arm, and pulling her away. "She's mine!" He growled, "She belongs to me, and I won't let another man claim her!" With that, he let out a low, dominant growl, before quickly sinking his fangs in deep into her throat, clutching her tightly as blood flowed in like a dam into his eager mouth.

Asuka finally let out a scream that ripped from her throat. Her eyes were shut tight as his nails dug into her skin, pulling her closer to him. Her mind swam as it began to fade, then all went black.

***

Meagen's eyes went wide as she heard the scream, echoing all around the hollow, empty grounds. She bowed her head, putting on another burst of speed. "Hurry up!" She exclaimed.

Cyrus and Cyro both ran ahead, both emitting low, feral growls, as if to say, "Bring it!"

Lilan panted, trying to keep up, "You think that was Asuka?"

Meagen nodded, "Sure of it!" She growled, "Forget it! This form is taking too long!" She ripped off her shirt, throwing it to the ground. She leaned forward onto her hands, the change rapidly going through her body. Fur, black as the night, began to sprout everywhere, covering her body as her clothes slipped easily off her agile form. Her muzzle grew out, making her shiver in delicious delight, as she enjoyed the transformation. Her tail shot out, sleek and smooth under the starlight. Meagen let out a low, long howl, signaling the end of the transformation. She put on another burst of speed, blending in with the shadows.

Cyrus and Cyro let out surprised barks, both trying to catch up with her.

Sofy came up to Lilan, eyes wide, "So, Meagen was a hybrid this whole time?"

Lilan nodded, "Yeah!"

Cloe came up to Lilan's other side, panting as she tried to keep up,."So, why did she lie about her species?" She asked.

Lilan narrowed her eyes. "Because she wasn't injected with vampire or lycan venom, " She said, "Her mother was a vampire, her father a lycan."

Sam nodded in understanding. "But why the secrecy?" She wondered aloud.

Lilan sighed, "Because her father used to work under Xanatos, while her mother was a slave dancer. They met during the time her mother was just brought in, both had fallen in love, and mated, giving birth to a hybrid." Lilan growled, "Xanatos saw Meagen as a tool, and raised her to be a sex toy, so to speak."

Sam narrowed her eyes. "So she was afraid to trust anyone, due to the fact that she might have been sold out to Xanatos." She said, bowing her head, "The poor child."

Meagen stood up ahead, looking regal in the moonlight. She barked once, but everyone understood the meaning.

They had arrived, and death already hung over the air.

***

Thane eagerly drank from her arched throat, holding tightly onto her. Asuka started going numb as Thane growled, taking more from her body.

Yes, The voice hissed in his head, *Kill her, Thane. Drain the slut slowly until she's dead.*

Thane! Another voice in his head shouted, *Snap outta it! You're killing the one girl you love, and you don't even realize that!*

Shut up! The woman hissed, anger in her voice, *Thane, ignore the other voice, and finish her!*

No! The other voice howled, *Please, Thane, wake up and come to your senses! Thane!*

Shut up, the both of you! Thane thought, anger flooding through him, as he bit down harder on Asuka, making her jerk in response, *Go away, the both of you! Now! I do what I want, when I want! So butt out!*

Just kill her, and be done with it! The woman growled.

The other voice let out a snarl, anger rising in his voice, *Thane, you idiot! Open your eyes! You're killing Asuka! Please, listen to me! You have to snap out of it! Thane!*

Thane's eyes snapped open, the voice screaming in his ears. He paused, taking in slow, even breaths. Slowly, his surrounding came back into place, clear as crystal. He and Kursed were in an empty room, Kursed playing decoy to lure Asuka inside. They had both fought, and Thane had interrupted the killing blow, eager to rip out Asuka's own throat with his own fangs. He had been so close to killing her, to tasting her blood again.

I love you

Those three words echoed over and over again in his head, surprising him. Kursed had tried to steal Asuka away from him, to kill her himself. Anger had flooded from within Thane, drowning out all other emotions. He felt anger at Kursed, for trying to steal Asuka away. And anger at Asuka, for not even fighting back. The important thing was, though, that Thane wanted Asuka all to himself, blood, body, and soul.

Thane remembered reaching out and pulling Asuka away, wanting to claim her for his own. He had felt her fear, of course. But there was something else that was there, beginning to show through, bravery. Asuka would not fight back, not against the ones she cared about.

And Thane had carelessly thrown her feeling for him away, to follow the orders given by a filthy tramp, just to shut her up.

Kursed placed a gentle hand on Thane's shoulder, lightly shaking him, "Thane, let her go, please."

His voice was so calm, free of the coldness that Kursed had held earlier. But there was a bit of sadness in his voice, as he tried to hold back the raging emotions he held within him. He looked down at Asuka, eyes filling with unshed tears. "Please," He whispered, voice choked.

Thane tensed, feeing his teeth embedded in flesh, blood slowly filling his mouth. He slowly pulled away, licking his lips clean. He looked down at Asuka, hoping against hope, he wouldn't see what he thought he would.

Asuka's head laid at an angle, two semi-large holes in her throat. Twin rivers of blood oozed down her arched throat. Several claw marks bled in her arms, more evidence of his brutality. "Asuka," Thane whispered.

Ivory was trying to reach him again, screaming in anger as his mind blocked any and all entry, keeping her out. Ivory was upset, raging in his head, but he ignored it, knowing full well she didn't have a hold of his mind anymore. Gently, lovingly, he touched her cheek, trying to rouse her. "Come on, Asuka, wake up," Thane breathed, eyes wide as his heart froze over, "Asuka, please, wake up."

Asuka did not stir, nor did she show any sign of waking. Tears filled his eyes as they fell silently down his cheeks, blood red against his skin. Thane raised a hand up, wiping them away. He was still in shock over his tears. Tears! In all of his lifetime, not once had he shed a single tear. Now, he knelt beside the one girl he had promised to protect, who had put all her trust and faith into him, grieving over her death. A death he had brought by his own hands.

Thane swallowed, mouth suddenly dry, "Kursed...I'm sorry. I...I just lost control."

Kursed nodded slowly, "We...we both did. Thane, we were being controlled, given orders to kill her."

Thane snarled, fangs bared, "We could have fought it! Asuka didn't have to die!" He growled, anger flooding through him, "Xanatos! This is all his fault! I'll kill him!"

Kursed gripped his arm. "Thane, wait!" He said, "What about Asuka? We need to try and help her."

"What do you suggest we do?" Thane growled.

Kursed met his gaze, the same emotions reflecting in his own eyes, "We can sire her."

Thane shook his head, "It might not work."

Kursed placed a hand on his shoulder, "We can only try. Thane, please, there still might be a chance."

Thane bit his lip, before nodding, "Keep lookout."

Kursed nodded, "Will do!" He hurried over to the door, barely breathing as he stood still, eyes continuously searching.

Thane turned back toward Asuka, easing her up into a sitting position. He quickly bit his lip, pressing them to her own numb ones, pushing with his tongue to keep them open. He quickly tried to press his lower lip to her, trying to get the blood inside her. Asuka's skin was beginning to cool with traces of death.

Growling in frustration, he pulled away. He swiftly sliced into his own wrist, and holding her head still, he pressed his wrist there. The blood passed through her numb lips, sliding down her throat and spreading through her body. But Asuka still refused to still, body limp in his arms.

After some time, Thane pulled his wrist away, feeling defeated. He gently placed Asuka back against the ground, letting her lay there by his knees. A few seconds later, Thane let out a snarl, scrambling to his feet. "I'm going to kill Xanatos!" He growled.

Kursed nodded, "Kinda figured."

Thane let out a breath, eyes hard, "You with me, friend?"

Kursed nodded, "Always, friend."

Thane smirked, before letting out a low growl, falling to his hands and knees. Dirty blonde fur began to sprout everywhere, muscles rippling through the clothing, shredding them as he groaned. His eyes flashed several colors, yellow, green, grey, black, then back to yellow. Adrenaline rushed through his body as his muscles grew out, growls thundering from within. His spine snapped into place as his tail grew out. Finally, Thane let out a loud, dangerous howl as his transformation finished. In his place stood a large wolf, growling in anticipation, eyes narrowed.

Kursed smiled, "You ready, Thane?"

Thane nodded, eyes slowly fading to grey. Kursed smiled, "Good. Now, let's go."

***

Ivory let out a small growl as she had receded from both the minds of Thane and Kursed. She was weak and exhausted, needing sustenance. She rammed a fist into a nearby wall, fury making her see red, pure crimson red. "Arrogant little mutts!" She snarled, "How dare they disobey me!"

Xanatos turned around, eyes wide as he twitched nervously, "They what?"

Ivory let out a small squeak as she froze, eyes wide. "Who did what?" She asked, giggling nervously.

Xanatos snarled, "Don't give me that bull!" He gripped her arm, "Now, tell me what happened!"

Ivory pulled away, breathing hard. "Thane and Kursed both broke the hold I had over them, and now they're coming here!" She growled, "And they're both pissed!"

Xanatos shook out of anger, eyes wide. He angry slammed his fist into the altar beside him, "Wonderful! What about the girl?"

"Dead," Ivory said, Apparently, Thane couldn't control his urges, or his sanity He fed from Asuka and drained her in the process."

Xanatos let out a howl of rage, "And did you not have the ability to stop them, or did your jealousy get the better of you?"

Ivory sputtered, crimson eyes glowing in anger, "What was she to you, huh? She was a little tramp who deserved what she got!"

"She was our ticket to defeating the rebels!" Xanatos snarled, "I was to use her blood to gain power, and to summon the Shadow Lord. From there, it was to feed off of Asuka!" He growled, "It was supposed to kill anyone who got in its way!

Ivory shied back, eyes wide, "How was I supposed to know, master?"

Xanatos growled, "It doesn't matter now."

Ivory shook her head, "Why now?"

He sighed, "Because, we have company."

The double doors smashed open, revealing a dirty blonde wolf, snarling and baring his teeth. Kursed stood next to him, eyes wide with amusement. "Thane, do me a favor, alright?" He said, voice calm and steady. The large wolf looked up at him, waiting for a response. Kursed smiled, showing his fangs, "Sic 'em!"

Thane snarled in response, leaping forward, and slashing into anything within reach of his claws. Ivory tried to lash out with her boot, but Thane snapped at him, teeth clicking on air. He spun around, growling as he advanced closer on Ivory, waiting for her next move.

Kursed rushed at Xanatos, nails raking against his face. Xanatos snarled, holding his bleeding cheek, feeling it begin to heal. He chuckled, eyes flashing, "Was that it, child?"

Kursed chuckled, "I'm just getting warmed up." He lifted up his foot, aiming a kick for his head. Xanatos grabbed his foot, twisting it to the breaking point. Kursed howled in pain as he fell to the ground, holding his ankle.

Xanatos advanced on him, chuckling, "You're merely a child, Kursed, trying to play with the big kids."

Kursed shook his head quickly, "If I'm the child, what does that make you?"

Xanatos smiled, "Someone who wouldn't let his girlfriend come up here, that's for sure." He chuckled, "And it seems Meagen is here, heading to this room right now."

Kursed's eyes widened, "Meagen, no!" He scrambled to his feet, hurrying for the ruined door.

Xanatos growled, sidestepping him and quickly stabbing him in his stomach with a small knife hidden up his sleeve. Kursed howled in pain, dropping to his knees, while his blood poured into his hands. Xanatos smirked, "Oh, come on, Kursed, get up. Get up and fight me."

Thane turned away from the fight with Ivory, yelping in surprise. He ran forward, hurrying to his side. Ivory slipped an arm out, hitting him in the throat. He dropped to the ground, gasping for breath.

Xanatos smiled, "How does it feel to lose, you two? Bitter, cold? How about worthless." He looked at Ivory, "Anyone who comes in here, kill them. I've got to light the circle of candles."

Ivory smiled, "With pleasure!"

Thane and Kursed could only watch, pain numbing their bodies, as everything they had worked for, was about to now be destroyed. Thane reached out, snagging Ivory's boot with his teeth, digging in through the leather.

Ivory growled, "Let go, mutt!" She kicked him in the face, making him cry out in surprise, pain jolting through his body.

Ivory smiled, eyes filled with amusement, "Aw, did that hurt? Good. I want you to suffer." She cocked her head as her eyes twinkled in joy, "I think your friends have arrived. Time to go play."

***

Her body was on fire, as she convulse and twitched at the same time. She threw her head back, letting out a small growl. Her eyeteeth extended, revealing fangs, pushing through her gums. Her hands twitched, fingers bending like claws. She let out a scream, followed quickly by another as her throat burned like fire. God, the pain was intense, making her shudder as she went numb. Finally, the waves of pain subsided, reduced to a small, dull throbbing.

She sucked in a breath, eyes snapping open. Her master needed her. Slowly, she sat up, getting to her feet. Her master called for her, willing her to come. He was in pain, weak from blood loss.

She obliged, heading out the door.

***

Soft growling led Ivory to look over to the smashed door, seeing three large wolves standing there. The lithe one stepped forward, baring her teeth as she let out one long, low howl, urging the other wolves forward. Both Cyrus and Cyro leapt forward, teeth flashing.

A larger wolf leapt forward, yellow eyes glinting with hunger. A silvery, puffy X sat around her neck, while her paws remained white. Her fur was a darker silver, almost looking grey. She snarled, as if in challenge.

Cyro stepped forward, ears pressed back as he growled a warning growl, baring his teeth. He rushed forward, sinking his teeth into her left shoulder blade, tasting rich, coppery blood. Cyrus danced to Aurana's right, and snapped at her paws, driving her into a corner.

Aurana snarled, reaching over and latching onto Cyro, tasting blood. Cyro yelped, trying to pull away. Cyrus took his chances and leapt up, burying his muzzle into her thick, silvery pelt, growling as his teeth sank deeper and deeper.

Meagen ran up next to Kursed, nuzzling his face and whimpering softly, trying to rouse him. His eyelids fluttered opened, trying to focus. "M-Meagen?" He choked out.

She nodded, eyes wide. She let out a small warning growl as a shadow loomed over them. Kursed whirled around, lashing out with his foot. Xanatos snarled, clutching his throbbing jaw. Meagen leapt behind Xanatos, growling softly as she advanced.

Xanatos chuckled nervously, eyes wide, "N-now, Meagen, I'm sure you're probably pissed about what I did to your parents."

She snapped at one of his hands, making him jump in response. She advanced still, growls growing louder.

Xanatos slowly stepped forward, "But…that does not mean we can't start anew, and try again." He reached out quickly, gripping the scruff of her neck, and lifting her up, "But, of course, that's just an idea."

Meagen snarled, eyes livid as she struggled. She growled, pretty much telling Xanatos to do something anatomically impossible with himself as she bared her teeth in response. Xanatos simply chuckled, tossing her aside.

Thane watched as Meagen was thrown back, landing hard against the opposite wall. He shook his head, turning back to Ivory, shadows rising off of his paws. They seemed to rise like little fires around his body. A snarl ripped from his throat, growing louder by the second. Ivory froze, eyes wide, as she tried to look for a way out, a way to escape. She dodged for her left, but Thane beat her there, snapping down on her hand.

She howled in pain, holding her bleeding hand as she glared at him. "Great, Thane," She growled, "So, how are you going to kill me, huh? The same way I killed your little boy?"

Thane snarled, baring his teeth, as if to say, "Shut it!"

Ivory laughed, "Did I hit a nerve just now?" She began to circle him, eyes never leaving his own. She chuckled, "Where to begin with that one? Oh, I know!" She clapped her hands together, "Let's start with how I lured him out. It was pretty easy. All I had to do was imitate his precious little girl."

Thane let out a growl, reaching out to snap at her, which made Ivory laugh.

Ivory put on a simpering look, lips pulled into a mocking pout, while her voice changed pitch, becoming higher. "Help me, someone, please!" She mocked, "The creatures have me surrounded! I can't escape them! Someone, help! They're hurting me!" She cackled, "You should have seen his face when he saw me, instead of that simpering little brat."

Thane let out a loud snarl as he leapt up, knocking Ivory down. She screeched, raising her arms up to protect her face. Thane bit and scratched every bit of skin he could find, seeing red, bright, crimson red.

Xanatos turned around from his fight to see Ivory pinned to the ground, bleeding from multiple gashes all over her body and arms. He raised a an arm up, bringing it down toward Thane's head. Thane managed to look up in time to see the arm coming down.

A slim hand reached out, gripping Xanatos's arm, holding him in place. The newcomer chuckled, "Sorry I'm late, boys and girls."

Her name screamed in his Thane's mind as he let out a yelp of surprise, *No way! Asuka's alive!*

Chapter 20

Ivory swallowed a curse, eyes blazing, "I thought my men killed you, you little tramp!"

Asuka flicked back a strand of her hair, grinning slyly, "Guess you didn't count on the fact that they actually cared, deep down, past all the mind control and stuff, and that they wanted to save me." She winked slyly at Thane.

There were several loud sounds as Thane let out a low groan, losing the fur and muzzle, returning back to his human form. He smirked at Asuka, "Just wait, you'll love your lycan form."

Asuka smiled, "I kinda figured." She adverted her gaze, "But, Thane, some clothes?"

Thane smiled, "Am I distracting you?"

Asuka pretended to think for a moment, before shrugging, "No, not really. If we weren't in a dangerous situation right now, I might have enjoyed it. But you may catch a draft after awhile."

He nodded, "You're right." He looked around, "Anyone bring any spare clothes with them?"

Lilan ran over to him, holding a bundle of clothes in her small arms. "Right here!" She chimed out, "Lilth said she had a feeling you'd need them, and she was right!"

He took the clothes from her arms, smiling. "I'll be right back," He said, slipping into the shadows.

Asuka rolled her eyes, "Wonderful, pretty boy left."

Lilan looked up at her, eyes now ice blue and full of excitement. She moved a strand of now silver hair away from her face, "Yeah, but he'll be back." She giggled, "Thane loves to fight, and thrills for the kill when in a good enough mood."

Asuka grinned, "You take Ivory's left, I take Ivory's right?"

Lilan nodded, "I'm game! Let's do it!"

They rushed forward, quicker than the normal eye could perceive. Asuka raised a clawed hand up, aiming for Ivory's face, while Lilan slid one of her legs in an arc, slamming into Ivory. Ivory fell hard to the ground, body jerking in pain.

Ivory shot them a murderous look, crimson eyes wide, "You think you're so clever, working together, don't you?"

Lilan growled, "Silver, go! Freeze her!"

Ivory reached out, gripping Silver's tail, and throwing him aside, "Is that all you children got? Small attacks?"

Asuka launched forward, slashing Ivory's cheek. Four, long, jagged cuts ran down Ivory's face, bleeding freely. She glared at Asuka, "You've got some nerve, slut!"

Asuka smiled, "Did that hurt, Ivory?"

Ivory growled, lashing out at Asuka, and pinning her down. Raising her hands, she clasped them around Asuka's throat, and slowly began cutting off oxygen to her body. Asuka struggled, but Ivory straddled her, preventing escape. Ivory smiled, "Go ahead, call out for your friends. Show me your weakness."

A hand came down, gripping Ivory's hair, and slowly pulling her back, bringing her face to face with Thane. He growled, "Touch her again, and I'll slowly break every bone in your pathetic body."

Ivory growled, lashing out at him. Thane dodged, chuckling, "Is that all you got, little one? Come on, Ivory! Attack me like you mean it! Otherwise, I may just get bored with this, and kill you now."

Ivory reached into her boot, throwing a small dagger at him, "You can go burn for all I care!"

Thane deflected the blade, coming closer to her. He brought up his hand, creating several small, black daggers. Quicker than the normal eye, he threw them toward her. Each tiny blade grazed her skin drawing blood. She hissed in pain, stumbling a bit from blood loss. "Enough, m-mutt," She gasped out, "Can't we c-c-call a truce?"

Thane slowly shook his head, "Not until one of us is dead, Ivory."

Ivory curled her lip, "Until one of us is dead. So be it, mutt."

They both came rushing at each other, clawing and biting any spot they could find, drawing blood that shone in the dim light. Ivory bit down hard on his arm, growling like a wildcat. Thane let out a small growl as he gripped her hair, ripping her away. Thane snarled, "That's more like it."

Asuka could only watch for a second, until a large blade came down upon her head. She dodged, raising a foot up, and kicking the blade away. Xanatos growled in surprise, watching the blade clatter to the ground meters away. Raising her foot again, she launched it forward, slamming him hard several times in his jaw. His head snapped back as he bit down on his tongue, tasting blood. Xanatos could feel his nose shatter under her assault, blood oozing down his face.

Asuka brought her fist back, ready to shove it through his chest. Xanatos reached out, gripping her arm in an iron grip. Quickly, he lashed out with a small knife from his belt, slicing swiftly around her middle. Asuka cried out, dropping to her knees in unbridled pain. She looked up to see Xanatos raising the blade up, smiling. He swiftly raised the knife up, wiping it against the palm of his hand, and pressed it against the small altar, making it glow an unearthly color.

Everyone went silent for a moment, listening intently as they heard a small rumbling sound. Xanatos began to laugh insanely, "Finally! The beast has awoken! We can finally be in control!"

Ivory took her chance, while Thane kept his eyes on the altar, to run to her master, clutching his arm, "M-master, are you sure about this? This…this feels wrong."

Xanatos chuckled at her cowardice, "Better to wipe out all rebels here and now, then to take them out later, one by one."

Ivory growled, "I'd rather kill my enemy by my own hands, then to let some creature do my dirty work for me."

Xanatos reached out and smacked Ivory hard across her face. He growled, "I don't care about how you feel about this, Ivory. As I've stated before, I have no further use for you."

Her eyes widened, "Master, you don't mean that!"

Thane held her back, "Ivory, it's too late! He's already made his decision!"

"No!" She howled, breaking away from Thane and running to Xanatos, "Master, you can't mean that! Please!"

Thane reached out and gripped her tighter, "Ivory, please!"

Ivory thrashed and howled as blood red tears ran down her face, smearing her cheeks. Everyone could only watch in horror as something huge began to rise from the shadows. Long, spindly arms began to pull a large, slim creature out into the open. Darkness began to settle onto the bones, creating skin. Its skin was smooth, and black as the night. Four horns came out of its head, long and crooked. It opened its eyes, which were a deep, dark blood red. It slowly flexed its hands, claws long, looking in sad need of a trim. It threw its head back and roared, long and dangerous.

Xanatos smiled, eyes wide, "Welcome, oh mighty one!" He threw an arm toward Thane and Asuka, "Now, I want you to destroy those two, along with anyone who gets in your way!"

The creature looked down at Xanatos, snarling. Inside its mouth were rows and rows of razor sharp teeth. "You think you can tell me what to do?" It asked, voice deep and raspy, "You are an insignificant creature who barely has any place in this world. You, like so many who have walked these lands."

Xanatos growled in response, "Nevertheless, I summoned you. My words are your orders!"

The creature laughed, deep and reverberating, "Like I said, an insignificant creature who has no place in this world." It thought for a moment, looking away, "Still, to stay in this world, I will need a body." It smirked, "I supposed yours will do."

Xanatos took a step back, eyes wide, "You...you can't be serious!"

The creature laughed, "I'm always serious, blood worm." It chuckled as the shadows began to rise around them, concealing them both. Xanatos let out a loud scream of panic as the creature rushed toward his body, beginning to merge with him. Xanatos turned this way and that as his veins bulged, pulsing as he screamed again. He clutched his head as his body convulsed again and again, finally settling.

Xanatos grinned as he flexed his hands. "Well now, seems like this body is a perfect fit," He said, voice now slow and relaxed, "Thank you, *master.*" He chuckled in thought.

Ivory slid out of Thane's grip, falling to her knees, "M-master, why?"

Xanatos turned an eye toward Ivory, lip curled into a snarl, "Who are you again? You don't look familiar."

Ivory's jaw dropped, eyes wide, "M-master…no…"

Xanatos threw an arm out, chuckling, "Everyone attack!"

Lycans snarled, rushing forward, along with the vampires. There were horrible sounds of ripping and snarling, followed by fallen screams. Asuka stepped up next to Thane, raising both hands in defense, "What's the plan?"

Thane let out a small growl, eyes narrowed, "Attack, that's about it."

Xanatos chuckled, "You really think you can stop me?" His laughter grew, "Don't be ridiculous!"

Thane smirked, "Wanna bet?"

Xanatos paused, lightly sniffing the air, "I smell…one of pure blood." He turned his narrowed eyes to Asuka, tongue flicking over his lengthened canines, "One whose blood I need to survive."

Thane reached out, bringing his knees up, and slamming it under his chin. Xanatos howled in pain, holding his jaw. Thane smirked, "You'll have to get past me, first, unless it's too much of a hassle now."

Xanatos snarled, reaching out for Thane. Thane smirked, lashing out with his foot again. Taking a chance, he held out his hand, summoning a rather large, black blade. On the handle was a single, red ribbon, dangling a bit. Thane smiled, holding the blade with both hands, ready to attack, "Come and get us, already."

Xanatos snarled, rushing toward them. While they were fighting Xanatos, everyone else was busy dodging claws and feet, breathless, as more and more attacks came across them. Asuka could only watch, to provide back up, in case Thane needed it. Thane growled, swinging his blade down upon Xanatos.

Lilan and Sofy were dancing left and right as a rather slim vampire rushed toward them, screeching in anger. Sofy swept her legs toward the vampire, knocking her over. Lilan growled, reaching out, and snapping its neck. She smiled, "Thanks, Sofy!"

"No problem!" Sofy said, smiling.

Cyrus and Cyro had already partnered up to take down Aurana, who was cornered. Her ears sat back, growling in anger. Both twins took their chance, to snap at her paws. They seemed to be enjoying themselves. Aurana tried to snap back, but they both reached forward, not giving her a chance.

Kursed and Meagen stood back to back, fighting a couple of lycans. A lycan leapt up, ready to sink its teeth deep into Kursed's throat. Kursed ducked, allowing Meagen to leap up, gripping its throat, and quickly snapping its neck between her jaws. There was a loud crack, followed by silence. Meagen threw the lycan aside, growling for more.

Cloe and Sam were making short work of any vampires that came their way. Cloe slipped behind one, and leapt onto its back. Sam rushed at them, slashing at whatever she could. There were several loud cries as the vampires fell, one by one. They twitched, followed by stillness.

Asuka stared back at Thane, who was fending off all attacks from Xanatos. Blow by blow landed across his large blade. Thane growled, "Asuka, could use some help, over here!"

Asuka nodded, "Right!" She ran forward, jumping up behind Xanatos, and latching onto his neck, sinking her fangs in deeper and deeper as she tasted warm, coppery blood. Her eyes went wide as she growled loudly. Xanatos snarled, grabbing her by her hair, and yanking hard. Asuka jumped, biting down harder, but not letting go.

Thane took a chance to swing his blade down upon Xanatos, aiming for his head. Xanatos reacted, bringing a foot up, and kicking the blade away. Thane reached out, trying to grab the handle, "Asuka, cover me!"

She growled in response, letting go of Xanatos and facing his front. She brought her knees up, slamming it directly into his ribs, which cracked a few on impact. Xanatos snarled in pain, growling a curse or two. Asuka scrambled to get the knife left abandoned by his feet. Noticing her movements, Xanatos reached down toward his foot, but missed. Asuka managed to grab the knife and began to thrust it up toward his chest.

Xanatos gripped her wrist and twisted it, breaking a few of the bones. Asuka gritted her teeth, and tried to push her arm up, still gripping the blade. Xanatos smiled, twisting the blade around, and started to bring it down upon her slowly, grinning insanely.

He chuckled, "After I've stabbed you, I'll drain all your blood, and use your body as one of my puppets." The knife started to pierce through her chest, drawing blood. He sniffed deeply, bending down to lick away some of the blood that dripped down her front, "You taste so delicious, Asusu."

Asuka tried to push it away, but felt her wrist start to give. "Thane!" She cried out, "A little help here!" The blade started to push more through her skin, drawing more blood. She let out a loud cry, "Please!"

The black blade started to fall upon a quick arc down toward Xanatos, aiming for his exposed throat. With a quick whoosh, the blade sliced cleanly through his neck, head toppling freely off. Silently, Xanatos fell on top of Asuka, blood flowing like a waterfall, coating everything in its path. Asuka screeched loudly, covering her face as she could smell the coppery substance, almost tasting it on her tongue.

Thane scrambled to get near Asuka, pulling her hastily out from under the body. Within seconds, the body burst into black, suffocating flames. Ivory watched in horror as the flames consumed his flesh, turning it black. "Master!" She cried out, voice choked with emotion.

She tried to run toward Xanatos, but was restrained by Kursed. "Enough!" He exclaimed, "Xanatos is gone! There's nothing you can do now!"

"You're wrong!" She shrieked, looking at Kursed, "I can still help him! I have to help him! Someone, please, put out the flames!" She looked back at Xanatos, whose body started deteriorating, turning to ashes. Something flew through the room, scattering the ashes near their feet.

Asuka finally relaxed against Thane, slowly closing her eyes. "Is it over?" She whispered.

Thane nodded slowly, "Yes, I think it is, little Asusu."

Asuka snuggled against him, shaking from the cold, "Can we go home, now? Please?"

He nodded, "Yes, we can."

They stayed like that for a few minutes, until a soft rumbling started around them, followed by the smell of dust in the air. Asuka held on tighter to Thane, eyes wide, "Thane, what's going on?"

Thane shook his head, "I don't know!" He reached over to Ivory, gripping her hair tightly in his hand, "What's going on, Ivory?"

Ivory sniffled, blood red tears falling down her cheeks. "It was all Xanatos!" She cried out, eyes wide, "He had it all set up, to where if he died, this entire old castle would come down, burying any survivors!"

He threw Ivory aside, swearing under his breath. "Everyone, listen up!" Thane called out, "We have to leave this castle, now! Otherwise, we'll all be trapped. Those wishing to stay alive, you'll follow Asuka and myself. Those wishing to stay, then I wish you luck." He gripped Asuka's hand, and started pulling her along, small bricks fell down from the ceiling in their wake. Everyone quickly and calmly made their way toward the exit.

Dust rose into the air, choking Asuka as they ran. "Thane!" She called out, "There's so much dust! I can't see!" She coughed a bit, her mouth feeling dry as cotton.

"Just hang on!" Thane cried out, his grip tightening on her hand, as he continued to pull her along, "I've got you!"

Asuka felt her hand grow sweaty in his grip, slipping a bit, "Thane!" She fell backwards, landing hard on her side. More debris fell, piling up in the hallway. "Thane!" She cried out, "Where are you?" She got up from the ground, trying to avoid the debris. A brick fell down, knocking into her head.

Stars shone in her eyes as she stumbled, falling to the cold floor. She looked up in time to see a piece of debris come down upon her ankle, pinning her down. Asuka screamed in pain, as she heard a loud crack in the air. She cast a look down to see her ankle pinned. Slowly, it started to go numb, as exploding pain shot through her body. She tried to claw her way out from the debris, but everytime she moved, more pain shot through her. Her vision swam as tears came to her eyes, threatening to fall.

A figure came back through the debris, face chalky with dust. He knelt beside Asuka, moving hair out of her face. "Asuka?" he whispered.

Asuka blinked back bloody tears as she focused her vision, as she saw Thane, concern in his eyes. She smiled gently. "You came back," She whispered quietly.

Thane nodded, a gentle smile on his lips, "Yeah, I did." He shook his head, "Look, now's not the time to get sentimental. We gotta get you outta here!"

She tried to get up, but felt her ankle scream in pain. She let out a small noise, "Thane, I can't. My ankle is pinned."

He looked over at her ankle, seeing a rather large piece of brick trapping her. He met her eyes, gently touching her cheek, "I can get it off, but it may hurt."

Asuka gritted her teeth, "I'm used to pain by now."

"A normal feeling," Thane chuckled, reaching out and chucking the piece of debris away. He froze at the sight of her ankle, seeing a large black and purple bruise forming on her skin, along with several bumps here and there. He gently placed his fingers around the spot, trying to find any broken areas. Asuka howled as his fingers touched a certain spot in the center of the bruise.

Asuka whimpered in pain, breathing hard, "Guess it really is broken."

Thane gently scooped her up into his arms, holding her tightly, "Hang on, little Asusu, and close your eyes. You may feel sick, but this is probably the best way to go."

Asuka nodded, burying her face into his chest, while tightly clutching his shirt. Placing a hand on the back of Asuka's head, Thane closed his eyes, and let the shadows take them both. A cold, numbing sensation started to run through them, as their skin began to tingle. "Thane," Asuka called out, voice shaky, "I don't feel so hot." She gritted her teeth as she accidentally tapped her good foot against her bad one, pain shooting up and down her leg. Her stomach lurched as they continued to move through the shadows.

Finally, the two of them landed outside the crumbling fortress, sprawling onto the grass. Asuka got up onto her knees, and retched, expelling the contents of her stomach. She coughed a few times, before sitting back onto the grass, breathing hard.

Thane reached out to her, eyes wide, "Are you alright?"

Asuka turned her hazel eyes toward him, eyes that almost always seemed to make him melt from within, would make his bones turn to rubber and dance. She smiled, "Y-yeah, I am."

He let a slow smile grace his lips, eyes twinkling. He let out a genuine laugh, "That's good. I'm glad." He gently stroked her hair, feeling giddy with happiness, "Thank God you're alright."

There was a loud squeal as a figure with brown hair rushed forward, throwing Asuka into a tight embrace, "You're okay! You're actually okay, Asuka!"

Asuka gently laughed, holding Lilan close, "Yeah, I'm fine." She snuggled with Lilan as the small girl cried into her outfit, shaking, "When we didn't see you, Thane went back inside, determined to get you to safety." Lilan sniffled, "I thought you were dead."

Asuka gently shushed the small girl, chuckling softly. "It's alright, Lilan, I'm here," She crooned softly, "I'm not going anywhere."

Lilan nodded, "I don't want you to leave, promise me that. Please?"

Asuka nodded, "I promise, Lilan."

There was a silent whoosh of air as an arrow flew through the night, piercing through Asuka's chest. Her eyes widened in surprise as a blinding pain shot through her body. Slowly, she fell, breathing ragged and shallow as she tried to pull it out. Everyone whirled around to see a slender blonde girl, holding a crossbow, eyes narrowed in rage.

Asuka let out a small cough, blood oozing from her mouth, "E-Elora?"

Elora curled her lip in disgust, raising the crossbow again, "Good bye, tramp."

There was a small noise as Elora was taken down by a figure with flaming red hair. Asuka landed on top of Elora, knocking the crossbow aside. A low, dangerous growl escaped her lips, as she stared down at Elora. Asuka placed two hands on the sides of her head. "Good bye old friend." She whispered, grunting as she broke the blonde's neck. Elora twitched a few times, before going still, eyes wide and glassy.

Asuka let out a sigh, before getting off of Elora, staying on her knees. Thane ran over to her side, gently holding her up, "Asuka, come on, say something!"

She raised a finger, placing it gently against his lips, silencing Thane, "You did nothing wrong, Thane. You saved me."

Thane bit his lip, looking at the arrow. "Maybe we can pull it out," He said, reaching for the shaft and gently pulling it.

Her eyes went wide as pain lanced through her body, making her cry out, "Thane, stop it! That hurts! Please!"

His eyes went wide as he felt her skin. "Her body," He breathed, "It's losing heat!" He looked at the others, "We have to do something, now!"

Kursed fell beside Thane, voice strained with emotion, "I…I don't think there is a way, Thane. She's…almost too far gone."

Thane growled, "I won't lose her! Not like this!" He blinked back moisture that started to form in his eyes, "I can't!"

Asuka's eyes fluttered open, trying to focus. She gently placed a cold hand against Thane's warm cheek, gently smiling. "You won't lose me," She whispered, "I'll always be here." She coughed, pain jolting through her body, as she closed her eyes.

Thane let a howl escape him as anger started to rush through his body, "I need options! Please!"

Kursed bit his lip, drawing blood. "There are two choices," He said, "But they might now work."

Thane quickly nodded, "I'll do anything at this point."

Kursed cast a look at the arrow, "One, you can leave the arrow, and let her die here."

Thane growled, "And the second, Kursed?"

Kursed met his eyes. "You can break the arrow shaft," He held a hand up, "But, since it's so close to her heart, you can take the chance of piercing it."

"So she dies either way?" Thane snarled, "You know what? It's a chance I'm willing to take."

Kursed nodded, "Then, go ahead."

Thane nodded, turning back to Asuka. "This may hurt, Asuka," He said, "But it's the only chance we've got." He gripped the arrow tightly and bent the shaft, snapping it in half.

Asuka let out a loud scream, eyes wide as she sat up a little bit, before falling back against Thane, laying across his lap. Thane gently touched her face, trying to rouse her, "Asuka, come on, wake up."

There was no answer from her, as she laid quietly against Thane. All the lycans rose their heads up to the moon up ahead, and let out long, mournful howls. Each howl echoed the sounds of their breaking hearts.

Thane scooped Asuka up, and held her close, hoping to God she would survive. Slowly, his eyes fell closed, as he allowed himself to rest. He would wait for Asuka to wake up, for there still remained a small spark of life inside that beating heart of hers.

Epilogue

The music echoed all around the territory, loud and thumping enough to make the blood start to pump with adrenaline, making everyone dance. Outside, the lycans ran through the shadows, barking and howling or joy. Inside the mansion, lights flashed as multiple figures swayed with the beat.

A figure had just stepped outside to get some air, breathless with excitement, for once. Thane sighed, walking out into the small garden, "Little Asusu, you there?"

Out onto a small platform stepped a young girl with flowing red hair down to her back. Her hazel green eyes sparkled with unbridled amusement. Asuka smiled a small smile, "I'm here, Thane. Always will be."

Thane smiled, sliding a hand up to her cheek, "Why are you out here, away from the party?"

Asuka shrugged, "It was a bit too noisy for me, so I had to step out."

Thane laughed, slow and rich to her ears, "I can agree with you there." Thane reached over to one of the vines, and picked off a small, pink rose, and gently tucked it behind her ear, "There, a beautiful rose, for a beautiful girl."

Asuka blushed lightly, avoiding his gaze, "I'm not that beautiful."

Thane placed a gentle hand on her shoulder, slipping the other around her waist, "If you weren't beautiful, I wouldn't have claimed you for my own."

She rolled her eyes, "So, you wanted me because of my beauty?" She pulled out of his grasp, chuckling softly, "Tell me, Thane, what else do you like about me?"

Thane was taken aback for a moment, stammering a bit, "Um, w-well, let's see here. I know I can do this."

Asuka crossed her arms, waiting, "Well?" Thane didn't respond at first, which made her smile falter a bit. "You mean, you only chose me, because of my looks?" She asked, looking away, "Thanks a lot, Thane."

His arm slipped around her waist, pulling her close to him. "I chose you for more than that," Thane said, chuckling, "I chose you, because of your heart. You're kind and gentle to everyone."

Asuka smiled, "And what else?"

Thane placed a hand under her chin, and slowly lifted her face up. "I also like your eyes," He said softly, "The first time I saw them, I felt like I was falling into your soul. Your lips, because they're small and perfect. And lastly, your soul, because it's beautiful."

Asuka snuggled against him, content as a kitten, "Good to know you like me for me, Thane."

Thane smiled, "Wanna know something?" She nodded, "Before I met you, I was a cocky little prick with no emotions whatsoever. Sure, I got angry a lot, and used to smack around anyone who pissed me of. But since I met you, I've gotten a chance to change, to express myself." He gently kissed her lips. Finally, Thane pulled away, smiling, "I used to think showing any emotions was a sign of weakness, a sign that let your enemies know that they could get to you. Now I know I can show any emotion, because I know there will always be someone there, who will accept them, good or bad, no matter what."

Asuka met his gaze, eyes twinkling, as she nodded, "And I'll continue to accept them, as long as you and I live, and are together."

Thane met her lips with his, gently pulling her closer. A smile passed over Asuka's lips, as her hands ran themselves through his shoulder-length hair. After a few minutes, they pulled away, breathless. Asuka laid her head against his shoulder, sighing in content.

Thane smiled, "And you'll always be with me, for as long as I live and breathe."

Asuka nodded, "As will I, Thane."

Quick footsteps ran out toward the platform, startling them. Lilan stood there, breathless and wide-eyed, "Thane! Asuka! Thank God I've found you two!"

Asuka smiled gently, "What is it, Lil?"

Lilan cast her crimson eyes upon the two of them, taking in a deep breath, "Lilth wants to see you two. She says she has another assignment for you, and you need to get ready as soon as possible."

Manufactured By: RR Donnelley
                     Breinigsville, PA USA
                     November, 2010